"YOU GOT A BAD HABIT OF GOING FOR OTHER MEN'S MONEY," SLOCUM SAID.

"I wasn't cheating!" The gambler jumped up and reached inside his jacket. He pulled out a Colt .44 with its barrel sawed down to three inches.

He didn't get to use it. He was shot dead by Jed, the bouncer for the River Pilot Saloon.

Slocum had just won a $2000 pot. Keeping it from greedy Jed and his three shotgun-toting men wouldn't be easy.

Staying alive wouldn't be easy, either.

OTHER BOOKS BY JAKE LOGAN

RIDE, SLOCUM, RIDE
SLOCUM'S CODE
SLOCUM'S FLAG
SLOCUM'S RAID
SLOCUM'S RUN
BLAZING GUNS
SLOCUM'S GAMBLE
SLOCUM'S DEBT
SLOCUM AND THE MAD MAJOR
THE NECKTIE PARTY
THE CANYON BUNCH
SWAMP FOXES
LAW COMES TO COLD RAIN
SLOCUM'S DRIVE
JACKSON HOLE TROUBLE
SILVER CITY SHOOTOUT
SLOCUM AND THE LAW
APACHE SUNRISE
SLOCUM'S JUSTICE
NEBRASKA BURNOUT
SLOCUM AND THE CATTLE QUEEN
SLOCUM'S WOMEN
SLOCUM'S COMMAND
SLOCUM GETS EVEN
SLOCUM AND THE LOST DUTCHMAN MINE
HIGH COUNTRY HOLDUP
GUNS OF SOUTH PASS
SLOCUM AND THE HATCHET MEN
BANDIT GOLD
SOUTH OF THE BORDER
DALLAS MADAM
TEXAS SHOWDOWN
SLOCUM IN DEADWOOD
SLOCUM'S WINNING HAND
SLOCUM AND THE GUN RUNNERS
SLOCUM'S PRIDE
SLOCUM'S CRIME
THE NEVADA SWINDLE
SLOCUM'S GOOD DEED
SLOCUM'S STAMPEDE
GUNPLAY AT HOBBS' HOLE
THE JOURNEY OF DEATH
SLOCUM AND THE AVENGING GUN
SLOCUM RIDES ALONE
THE SUNSHINE BASIN WAR
VIGILANTE JUSTICE
JAILBREAK MOON
SIX-GUN BRIDE
MESCALERO DAWN
DENVER GOLD
SLOCUM AND THE BOZEMAN TRAIL
SLOCUM AND THE HORSE THIEVES
SLOCUM AND THE NOOSE OF HELL
CHEYENNE BLOODBATH
SLOCUM AND THE SILVER RANCH FIGHT
THE BLACKMAIL EXPRESS
SLOCUM AND THE LONG WAGON TRAIN
SLOCUM AND THE DEADLY FEUD
RAWHIDE JUSTICE
SLOCUM AND THE INDIAN GHOST
SEVEN GRAVES TO LAREDO
SLOCUM AND THE ARIZONA COWBOYS
SIXGUN CEMETERY
SLOCUM'S DEADLY GAME
HELL'S FURY
HIGH, WIDE, AND DEADLY
SLOCUM AND THE WILD STALLION CHASE
SLOCUM AND THE LAREDO SHOWDOWN
SLOCUM AND THE CLAIM JUMPERS
SLOCUM AND THE CHEROKEE MANHUNT
SIXGUNS AT SILVERADO
SLOCUM AND THE EL PASO BLOOD FEUD
SLOCUM AND THE BLOOD RAGE
SLOCUM AND THE CRACKER CREEK KILLERS

JAKE LOGAN
SLOCUM AND THE RED RIVER RENEGADES

BERKLEY BOOKS, NEW YORK

SLOCUM AND THE RED RIVER RENEGADES

A Berkley Book/published by arrangement with
the author

PRINTING HISTORY
Berkley edition/March 1988

All rights reserved.
Copyright © 1988 by Jake Logan.
This book may not be reproduced in whole or in part,
by mimeogrpah or any other means, without permission.
For information address: The Berkley Publishing Group,
200 Madison Avenue, New York, N.Y. 10016

ISBN: 0-425-10701-9

A BERKLEY BOOK ® TM 757,375
Berkley Books are published by The Berkley Publishing Group,
200 Madison Avenue, New York, N.Y. 10016.
The name "BERKLEY" and the "B" logo
are trademarks belonging to Berkley Publishing Corporation.

PRINTED IN THE UNITED STATES OF AMERICA

10 9 8 7 6 5 4 3 2 1

Special thanks to Dan Hillstrom for his invaluable assistance in supplying information about Fargo, ND, and Moorhead, MN

1

John Slocum gave his head a quick toss to get the lank black hair from his eyes. To some at the poker table in the Lost River Pilot Saloon it appeared to be a nervous gesture. Anyone looking into those cold, steady green eyes knew otherwise. Slocum fanned the cards and made sure of what he already understood.

The riverboat gambler seated across from him was cheating.

No one else in the game had noticed the shaved edges of the cards. Slocum's sensitive fingers had picked up the cheat immediately—and he had gone along with it for his own reasons. He had not won much, but he had won consistently as the card sharp primed him for the kill. Now the gambler with the greased-back hair, the sharp-tipped mustache, and the watery blue eyes thought he had his fish on the hook. Reeling John Slocum in would be more difficult than he thought.

The tension in the saloon grew as the pot mounted. Slocum paid no attention to the onlookers slowly drifting over from the bar. St. Louis had been good to him so far. The fancy burgundy coat he wore, the brocade vest, the tight black breeches, all bought with earnings from these poker tables. Slocum wasn't likely to give any significant portion of it back now.

Especially not to a card cheat.

"I'll have to see you, and buck it up another twenty

dollars." The gambler dropped a gold double eagle onto the table. Silence fell. Slocum kept his face impassive. To smile now might scare off the gambler.

Slocum studied the gambler, then decided nothing would get the man out of the game. Greed possessed him totally. He thought he had it won by dealing seconds using the shaved cards.

The gold coin's ringing had barely died down when Slocum said, "The pot's getting mighty rich." His eyes locked with the gambler's. Slocum had to give the man this much. He did not flinch. His returning gaze was bold. And why not? He thought—*knew*—he was going to be the winner.

"What'll it be? Fold?"

"I'll see the raise and test the water with a hundred." Slocum pulled a roll of greenbacks from his coat pocket. The broadcloth jacket once more hung properly, its line undisturbed by the tight wad of scrip. Slocum had a Confederate Army veteran's distaste for greenbacks; he preferred hard coin. But folding money had its place. To carry this amount of cash in gold and silver would have required a wagon and team.

The gambler's facade cracked for a brief moment. Then greed triumphed. He looked at his cards as if he had never seen them before and pursed his lips. "Well, it's looking as if the water is mighty deep in this harbor. Match your hundred and try another ... five hundred."

The crowd's silence turned to a collective gasp. The Lost River Pilot saw some high stakes games, but nothing like this. If Slocum called, over two thousand dollars in gold and greenbacks would be weighing down the felt-covered table.

"There any trouble here?" asked a burly man whose front tooth had been capped with gleaming gold. His belly hung out over a hand-tooled gunbelt and he had the look of trouble.

"No need to bother yourself, Jed," Slocum said,

nodding toward the saloon's bouncer. "Not unless there's something wrong with the cards."

The gambler looked from Slocum to the mean and massive Jed and back. His face turned pale. "What are you saying, mister? This is an honest game. You saw me cut open a brand-new deck before we started."

"I saw you switch decks. You got one in your pocket suspiciously like the one furnished by the saloon."

"You calling me a cheat? Come right on out and say it, if you are."

"Wouldn't think of it," said Slocum. His easy acceptance of the situation made the gambler swallow hard. The impassive mask had shattered and had been replaced by fear.

"Let's just pull back our bets and call it an evening," the gambler said, reaching for the pot to get his money back.

Slocum grabbed the man's wrist. "What kind of game is this? I want to finish the hand. Why don't you? You having second thoughts about betting so much?"

"Yeah, Slick," an onlooker said. "I never seen you back down on a hand before. What's wrong? Lost your nerve?"

Slocum shifted slightly in his chair and reached for his vest pocket. The gambler tensed, then relaxed when Slocum came out with a gold watch. Slocum thumbed the case open and looked at the face. A quarter to twelve. Inside the cover was a picture of his parents.

Slocum closed the watch case and slipped it back into his pocket. The watch was all he had to remember his brother Robert. Pickett's Charge had cost too many lives. One had been his brother's.

The movement had distracted the swindler. Every second they waited, the gambler came closer to turning tail and running for the hills.

"I'll call," said Slocum, wondering if he should buck up the pot another few hundred. He knew what the man's hand looked like long before the gambler dropped his full house, jacks over fives, onto the table.

A sigh passed through the crowd. Slocum sat unmoving. The gambler's lips pulled back in a broad grin. "Beat you this time, mister. Better luck next time."

Slocum grabbed the man's wrist with his left hand as he reached for the pot again. "You got a habit of going for other men's money." With his right, Slocum dropped the four treys and a king on top of the pot.

"You couldn't! I dealt you..." The gambler's voice trailed off.

"You sayin' you knew what you dealt?" asked Jed in a soft, dangerous voice. "I got a name for that. Cheating. You been cheating in the Lost River Pilot Saloon? Mr. Hicks don't like that and what Mr. Hicks don't like, I surely don't." Jed pointed toward the saloon owner, who dressed like an undertaker. From his vantage at the back table the owner motioned to his bouncer.

"I wasn't cheating. Honest, I wasn't." The gambler shot to his feet, overturning his wooden chair. It clattered to the sawdust-covered floor with a loud crash. The gambler's sudden movement reaching inside his jacket dislodged the pocketed honest deck of cards. They fluttered to the floor as the gambler pulled out a Colt .44 with its barrel sawed down to three inches.

He didn't get the belly-gun leveled before Jed's hand flashed to his pistol. The explosion beside Slocum's right ear deafened him, but Jed's quick draw saved him the trouble of using the twin-barreled derringer he had drawn from his boot top and aimed across the table at the gambler's chest.

The gambler stood for a brief second, a stupid look on his face as he stared at his belly-gun. He dropped to his knees, then fell face forward on the floor. Jed already had his pistol back in its holster and motioned for two barkeeps to get rid of the body.

The crowd began moving back toward the bar and

SLOCUM AND THE RED RIVER RENEGADES 5

new shots of whiskey and the watery beer the Lost River Pilot served. Slocum reached out to pull in the pot he had just won.

A meaty hand stopped him. "There's somethin' I got to know," Jed said, staring into Slocum's cold green eyes and not blinking. "How is it you came out with the winning hand, even when he was cheating?"

"Lady Luck sits on my shoulder sometimes," Slocum said.

"Reckon that might be true," Jed allowed. He pulled up the gambler's chair and sat down, his bulk causing the wood to creak in protest. "Then again, it might be more'n luck. It might just be that you was cheatin' *him*."

"'Can't cheat an honest man,'" Slocum quoted. He tried to decide what it would take to get out of the saloon without raising a big fuss. Jed didn't have the look of wanting more trouble. But he did have a gleam in his eye that Slocum had seen many times before.

The last time had been just a few minutes before the gambler got blown away for making his move against a man itching to ventilate him.

"Can't decide how I'm going to get this much money out of here without drawing attention," Slocum said. He pulled the gold in and dropped it into his pocket. The greenbacks were rumpled and stacked an inch thick on the table. He tapped the pile significantly. "Jed, can you figure how I might get my winnings out of here without any trouble?"

Jed licked his lips. "That pile's going to make a lump in your pocket. Every cutthroat along the wharf is going to see it."

"I figured that much." Slocum split the pile about fifty-fifty. He hated to part with what might amount to five hundred dollars, even if it was in Yankee greenbacks, but walking out of the saloon alive was worth it.

Slocum's eyes darted from Jed to the back door. The

two barkeeps stood there, bung-starters in hand. Those heavy mallets were no match for the Colt Navy Slocum had slung in a cross-draw holster, but the three men armed with shotguns who roamed the saloon were. And then there was Jed. The man looked like a wallowing hog, but Slocum had seen few men quicker on the draw. He decided he could take Jed, if it came to that.

The shotguns and the others in the saloon would make short work of him. The long-faced Mr. Hicks sat at his table and watched solemnly. In his day, Slocum had seen more cheerful undertakers.

"I don't reckon Mr. Hicks is interested how you keep the peace around the Lost River Pilot, is he?" asked Slocum.

"He cares. But not a whole bunch."

Slocum smiled crookedly and left the five hundred in bills on the table. A quick motion swept the rest off and into his coat pocket. "I'd offer to buy you a drink, but I see a friend beckoning to me."

Jed turned toward the swinging doors leading out onto Clayton Street. Slocum used this diversion to stand and get his coat swept back away from his Colt.

"So it seems," said Jed, looking back at Slocum when he realized he had been put in a bad spot. He slid the extortion money in front of him and quickly leafed through it. "Money's just not good, unless you live to spend it." He saw how Slocum had changed the odds. "Get on out of here. Don't reckon there'd be your kind of action after all that's happened. And that fellow *is* waiting for you."

To Slocum's surprise a short, swarthy man was motioning for him. He took the opportunity to get clear of what might otherwise become a bloodbath.

"Good night, Jed."

"Don't bother coming back, mister," the huge man said. "Mr. Hicks wouldn't like it." He thumbed the stack of greenbacks almost wistfully, then added, "Neither would I. Killing gamblers can be fun. Killing *you* would be a chore."

Slocum tipped his hat in Mr. Hicks's direction, then walked out of the saloon with a steady gait. He stepped onto the boardwalk and felt the fetid St. Louis summer air hit him like a body blow. A quick swipe removed the sweat from his forehead. He had avoided a gunfight with Jed. That alone made him the night's winner.

The weight of gold in his pocket and the press of greenbacks against his fingers made him a big winner. And it was about time. He had been on the trail too long, living off the land, barely surviving. He had spent the winter trapping for furs in the Wasatch Mountains above Salt Lake City. The vicious cold had made the trapping poor. He had come down into Mormon country with fewer than fifty average pelts.

He couldn't fault the Mormons for cheating him as they had. Their life along the banks of the Great Salt Lake wasn't any easier than his had been. Still, he had collected less than half what the furs were worth if he had brought them directly to St. Louis for sale.

Slocum pulled a fine Havana from his coat pocket and struck a lucifer. The bright flare died and he lit the cigar. He puffed deeply, letting the smoke sink into his lungs. He liked the taste better than the quirlies he had been smoking on the trail—when he'd been able to afford anything. The trip from Salt Lake to Denver had been uneventful. From Denver to St. Louis had been more to his liking.

He remembered with some fondness the small group of disillusioned settlers he had led back to Iowa and the farmlands they had deserted for the promised riches out West. Slocum sucked in more smoke and let it linger. One faltering pioneer lady in particular stuck in his mind.

Ivy Slates, her name had been. Her husband had died on the trip to Denver from Iowa. She had family in the

Midwest and wanted to return. The others in the small wagon train had other reasons, but Slocum had liked her the best. They had spent many nights under her wagon, locked in one another's arms, talking about civilized cities like St. Louis.

Ivy had stayed with her sister and two brothers in Iowa. Slocum had drifted into St. Louis by midsummer.

He swiped at the sweat once more. Not a breath of air stirred along the river front. In the distance he heard the mournful yowl of a paddlewheeler's steam whistle. Some activity up and down Clayton Street showed more promise for the dawn than it did now.

Slocum looked around for the swarthy man who had signalled him in the Lost River Pilot. He was nowhere to be seen. Slocum shrugged it off. If the man hadn't come in and mistaken him for someone else, Jed might have decided that all the winnings was better than half the paper money. For the world it had looked as if Slocum had an accomplice waiting.

Slocum had to laugh. Jed had been just as eager to avoid facing down Slocum as he was to keep from shooting the portly bouncer.

He finished his cigar, tossed it in a watering trough, and started down the boardwalk, his boot heels echoing hollow. St. Louis was a different river town from most. There might be action elsewhere, but along these darkened streets people had already turned in for the night. In New Orleans, midnight would mark the beginning of the most intense gambling and whoring and drinking.

"Sir! Please!" The voice came from an alleyway to his right. Slocum didn't break stride as he kept walking. The cutthroats along the waterfront used dozens of different ploys to rob the unsuspecting. Slocum moved his coat away from his Colt Navy and made sure the thong that usually hooked over the hammer was off. It was. He had removed it before entering the Lost River Pilot Saloon.

"Sir, I need to speak with you!"

The voice carried a hint of a French accent. Slocum looked around and made sure no one loitered nearby who would club him from behind. Only then did Slocum turn to face the man in the alleyway.

"What do you want?" he asked. The man, hidden in shadow, moved out so that Slocum got a better look at him. As he had expected, this was the same man who had been in the saloon.

"I saw the trouble in the Lost River Pilot," the man said. "I did not want to get involved."

Slocum nodded. The man was slightly built and had a disturbingly feminine look about him. His hands fluttered nervously at the ruffles bubbling up at his throat and made him look even more like a woman.

Slocum inhaled. The man even wore perfume. Slocum had nothing against bathing. He didn't rightly like being around others who failed to take at least one bath a week, but the man detaining him carried cleanliness to extremes.

"Sir, she wishes to see you."

"She?"

"Here." The man's hands fluttered like bony butterflies and produced a small envelope from the folds of ruffles. "She ordered me to give this to you."

"And?"

"And I am to wait for an answer."

Slocum's ears strained for sounds around him. Horses and a rattling wagon down Clayton Street were all he heard, other than the boisterous crowd inside the Lost River Pilot beginning to sing as the whiskey dulled their minds and inhibitions.

He reached behind him and found the thick-bladed knife sheathed there. When Slocum pulled it out, the messenger jumped back, his hands going to his mouth in a very womanly gesture. Slocum snorted in contempt. A quick slash with the knife opened the letter.

He held it up to catch the faint light from a distant gas lamp. The note had been written in a strong, precise woman's hand. He read the single line of the message, then sniffed appreciatively. The paper had been scented with perfume—a real womans' perfume.

All the note said was: "Mr. Slocum. Meet me in the warehouse at the corner of Clayton and Harbor Streets in one hour."

It was signed Claudette Durant.

"Your answer, sir?"

Slocum looked at the messenger and wondered why a woman allowed such a fawning, mincing sycophant around here.

"Who is Claudette Durant? I don't believe I've heard of her."

"Sir, please! Your answer!" The messenger looked around, his eyes growing wider as if he feared something—or someone. Slocum glanced over his shoulder. Two men left the office building across the street. They turned toward the Lost River Pilot and never gave him a second look.

"Tell Claudette Durant I'll think about it."

"Does that mean you will see her? Her plight is terrible, sir!"

"Just what trouble does she find herself in?" asked Slocum, but he found himself speaking to thin air. The messenger had slipped back into the shadowy alleyways. Slocum looked around and saw two more men leaving the office building. Whatever the small messenger feared, it centered in that building.

Slocum tucked the scented letter in his pocket next to the gold coins and sauntered across the street to read the sign on the office building.

"Mississippi Shipping," he read aloud. Slocum turned and walked off, shaking his head. He saw nothing sinister in the building. Many riverboat companies had offices along Clayton Street, and even more shipping agents frequented the area.

Still, the subtle scent of perfume on the letter and its terse, mysterious request intrigued him. He wasn't sure he would meet with the woman. Then again, curiosity burned within him. Who was Claudette Durant and what did she want of him?

2

John Slocum tried to forget the scrap of paper in his pocket. The elusive perfume drifting from the note kept his thoughts returning to the servant who had delivered the message—and the message's author.

He inhaled deeply. The perfume cut through the fish and wet wood odors of the river front. Slocum began walking to settle things in his mind. He had a pocket filled with gold and an inner pocket stuffed with greenbacks. After the terrible winter he had experienced trapping in the Utah mountains, St. Louis and summer had been good to him. With the money he had, he could do anything he wanted.

He leaned against a rotting piling and stared across the broad, gently heaving, muddy Mississippi River. Two paddlewheelers blew their whistles as they passed. The moonlight gave them enough light to keep moving, even though only the bravest—or most foolish—pilots worked after the sun set. It was too hard seeing the telltale ripples in the river that meant a submerged sandbar and possible disaster.

Slocum shook his head. New Orleans was a town he had grown to love. The all-high activity contrasted sharply with St. Louis. Too many people in this city were just passing through on their way West or up river or down. They stopped, they slept, they moved on. Nobody lived here, or so it seemed to him.

His attention turned to a steamboat gently rocking

against the pier. *Pride of Orleans* was written on its side in bright gilt paint that shone even in the pale moon. Some roustabouts worked to secure cargo at the front but even here, on the river where he most expected it, he found little movement.

No energy. Nothing happening. For all his luck in the Lost River Pilot and other saloons along the river front, Slocum was bored.

His hand touched the piece of paper in his pocket for the tenth time. He reached inside and withdrew it. His nose wrinkled at the fragrance. What woman wore this scent? Or did Claudette Durant only use it on letters to lure men? He read the terse note again and tried to get some meaning from it.

Life had not always been kind to him. John Slocum knew more than a little distrust, yet his curiosity began getting the better of him. He had nothing to gain by accepting this unusual invitation—and he might have everything to lose. He glanced around to be sure no one crept up on him.

He was alone on the dock.

Alone and bored.

On impulse, Slocum thrust the note back into his pocket and started walking briskly toward Harbor Street. It would do no harm to snoop around and see if someone laid a trap for him, though it was too elaborate a ruse for most of the cutthroats along the river. They would prefer to lay in wait and bushwhack him.

Slocum chuckled. Most of them weren't even able to write, much less think of using a foppish servant to deliver what might prove to be a love note.

Harbor and Clayton Streets crossed less than a quarter-mile from the Lost River Pilot Saloon. Slocum stepped into deep shadows and studied the lay of the land. He took in deep, slow breaths to keep calm. Everything about this meeting felt wrong. Still, the more he looked the less he saw.

14   JAKE LOGAN

Slocum scratched his head. The feeling refused to go away, but nothing peculiar drew his attention. The night rested as peacefully on these streets as it did over the Mississippi River and most St. Louis citizens.

He took out his brother's watch and looked at the time. Less than twenty minutes had passed since the servant had given him the note. Slocum put the watch back in his vest pocket, then checked his weapons.

The derringer rested firmly in his boot top. The large knife rested at the small of his back. And from its soft leather cross-draw holster, his dependable six-shooter promised instant death to anyone trying to ambush him.

Slocum stopped in the center of Harbor Street and strained his senses one last time. The feeling of danger had not passed, but curiosity grew when he saw the sign on the warehouse.

"Mississippi Shipping," he read aloud. The servant had been frightened of the men coming out of Mississippi Shipping's office across the street from the saloon. Yet Slocum was supposed to meet the servant's mistress in a warehouse owned by the same company.

Slocum went to the front door and tugged gently. Locked. He drifted along the brick wall as quietly as a shadow. A side door stood open a crack. Faint yellow light from inside spilled out across the boardwalk. Before going in, Slocum glanced up and saw the gibbous moon hanging just over the peaked warehouse roof.

He pushed open the door and slipped inside, his hand on the ebony handle of his Colt Navy. Two people spoke in whispers he couldn't make out. Slocum wended his way through the piles of crates and stopped just outside the circle of light cast by a single coal-oil lamp.

He recognized the foppish servant immediately. The man didn't see him, although he faced in Slocum's direction. The servant's full attention was on the woman who stood with her back to Slocum.

"Mrs. Durant?" Slocum said softly. Both the servant and the woman jumped, as if caught in some unnatural act. The woman spun, her hand going to her throat as consternation swept over her.

"Mr. Slocum? Is that you?"

"He's the one," the servant said. "He's the one you told me to give the message to."

"Yes, Pierre, thank you."

"Madame, please. Do not do this thing!"

"That will be all, Pierre." The woman's voice carried a steel edge that belied her beauty. Slocum appreciated the lustrous blonde hair piled high and dotted throughout with small pearls. A matching string dropped low under her neck and dipped down daringly low. The soft swell of her breasts rose from her stiff bodice and gratefully accepted the strand of pearls in the cleavage. The dress was of the finest lime-green velvet and trimmed with lace. She wore black silk gloves and clutched a tiny sequined purse.

From its heft, Slocum guessed she had a small pistol inside.

"I wasn't expecting you, Mr. Slocum. Not after what Pierre said in reply."

"I said I'd think about coming. I thought about it." Slocum looked around the warehouse and saw nothing sinister. The woman would have chosen a spot where she felt safe, if she wanted to hire him for something illegal—and Slocum would have bet most of the gold in his pocket that this was precisely what Mrs. Durant was going to propose.

"I'm sorry. Please, sir, be seated. The accommodations are not the finest, but it is necessary that I not be seen."

"Madame, please do not do this." The servant hovered at the edge of the small space formed by the mountains of crates.

"If you want to keep yourself busy," Slocum said to

the servant, "go and close the door. I saw this light from outside."

"Do as he says, Pierre. Now!" Again the hard edge came to Claudette Durant's voice. For all her delicate beauty, she was used to giving commands and being obeyed instantly. A cold iron core lay inside her.

Slocum sat with his back against a crate. From this position he could watch the approach of the door and keep anyone else from sneaking up behind him.

"I need your help, Mr. Slocum."

"I can't see why," he said. The light from the lamp cast shadows on Mrs. Durant's cheekbones, giving her an exotic and appealing look. He tried to guess how old she was. His first impression had been the twenties. Closer examination made him raise the guess to mid-thirties. She used her obvious wealth to maintain a youthful appearance with tailored clothing and facial makeup.

And she did it well. Slocum wondered what else she did well.

"It might seem that I can buy anything I desire," she said, a touch of bitterness in her voice. "That is true—except for one item I have come to value very much."

"And one which you do not have," said Slocum. He stood. He had no desire to engage in a treasure hunt for a spoiled rich woman.

"Wait, sir. Please. Hear me out. This one thing I do not have. It is not material. It is my freedom."

Slocum paused. He had not expected this. He, of all people, valued freedom above all else. Many times he had come close to losing it. A lump of bitterness formed and made him want to spit. He touched the watch in his pocket and remembered his brother Robert and his parents. They had died while he was recuperating after a serious wound given him by Bloody Bill Anderson after Quantrill's Lawrenceville raid. He had returned to Calhoun County, Georgia, and found the Slocum family farm all his.

He had worked it well until a carpetbagger judge had taken a shine to the place. The judge and his hired gunman had ridden in one afternoon, thinking they would seize it for back taxes that had never been paid—or owed.

Slocum had ridden away that evening. The new graves stood on the ridge by the spring house. Slocum had run from the charge of judge killing for years. He knew how fragile and precious freedom was.

"You look free enough to me, ma'am," he said. "Money buys many things. It can even buy freedom."

"I will pay you the sum of five thousand dollars to escort me to Fargo, in Dakota Territory."

"What?" Slocum shook his head. He couldn't understand what she wanted. He knew little of Fargo, save that it had been settled just before William G. Fargo of Wells, Fargo and Company fame brought in the Northern Pacific Railway. That had turned a sleepy little farming town of almost two hundred into a booming city of almost eight hundred. Why anyone, much less such a lovely and rich woman, would want to go there escaped him.

"We will take the *Pride of Orleans* north, port across on a rail spur, find another steamboat, follow the Red River to Fargo, and I will disembark there."

"How does this have anything to do with your freedom?" Slocum couldn't make head nor tail of what the woman was saying. "Looks as if all you want is someone to hold your hand. Wouldn't mind doing that, ma'am, since it looks to be a mighty fine hand, but—"

"Oh, you!" Claudette Durant stormed. She stamped her foot. The faint accent Slocum had detected before now came through strongly as French. "You know nothing of what I endure daily! You will accept my offer."

"Or I won't," said Slocum, irritated with the obstinate woman. He had money in his pocket. There was no need to put up with a strong-willed woman—and one who lost her temper easily. How she had chosen him out of all the drifters in St. Louis, he didn't know or much care. All Slocum could think of was that there were still saloons and casinos open somewhere in the city with drunks unable to calculate odds. He could make himself five thousand richer before dawn and not have to travel to far-off Fargo.

"You must. I beseech you!" She grabbed his hand and clutched it to her bosom. The woman's breast heaved under his hand. He felt the rapid beating of her heart, but this did not move him. With money in his pocket, he could have most any woman. Maybe they wouldn't be as pretty as Claudette Durant, but the bother wouldn't be as great, either.

"Why do you have to go to a godforsaken place like Fargo? That's in the middle of the prairie."

"There are docks on the Red River," she said. "They build barges. The city has many unique . . . attractions."

"Not for me. Good evening." He tipped his hat.

Before he got free of the woman's clutching hand, her servant cried out from his post at the door. "They come, Mrs. Durant. Four of them!"

"No!" Claudette Durant gasped. She bent over and extinguished the coal-oil lamp and rushed into the depths of the warehouse. Slocum started after her, then stopped. Whatever trouble the lovely woman was in, she had got there by her devices. It was a shame, he decided, but it was also none of his business.

Gruff voices sounded at the side door. One carried louder and more distinctly than the others. "He told us she'd be here. I can smell her goddamn perfume."

"That's her sissy servant. What's his name?"

"Why, Luke? You gettin' sweet on him? Want to kiss him? Just a little?"

Slocum heard the meaty thunk of a fist striking a

face. Angry curses erupted as the two men began fighting. The first voice shouted, "Knock it off, you two, or I'll have your balls nailed to the barn door. Dammit, the boss said she was in here. Find her!"

Slocum moved quietly through the warehouse. His eyes slowly adjusted to the darkness. He came to the front door and ran his fingers along the splintery doorjamb. He found the bar that had prevented him from entering earlier. Holding his breath, he lifted the bar away and put it down without a sound.

The door squeaked loud enough to wake the dead when he opened it. Slocum cringed, but there was nothing he could do about it. He pushed through and into the humid summer night air hanging along Harbor Street.

He saw no trace of Mrs. Durant or her servant. Slocum decided not to stay and find out if she had escaped the four men following her, though he felt a momentary pang at this. He knew nothing of the trouble the woman was in. It shouldn't concern him.

It shouldn't. But he still worried over her safety.

Slocum walked briskly up Harbor Street and turned down Jackson, intending to find a saloon with a decent poker game. It was only a little after one o'clock. He had most of the night ahead of him.

Gravel crunched behind him. Slocum spun, crouched, and drew his Colt. He saw only emptiness and shadow. Moving on cat-light feet, he ducked into an alley and waited to see who followed. His legs began to cramp after a few minutes. He straightened and put away his pistol, feeling foolish. He had started jumping at the slightest sound.

On impulse, though, Slocum cut down the first crossing street, paying no attention to direction. He walked randomly for several minutes, eventually finding himself once more on Clayton and near the docks. He doubled back, checked to see that no one trailed him, then began to curse his suspicious nature.

He didn't belong in the big city. Everyone was a potential thief or murderer here. The mountains hadn't given up their furry animal pelts easily last winter, but he had been where he belonged. With the money riding in his pockets, he could buy a horse and tack and ride back West. He had no business staying in St. Louis.

Slocum leaned against a piling and stared across the choppy Mississippi. The steamboats he had seen earlier were long gone. The *Pride of Orleans* still banged gently against the pier, but its crew had gone to sleep for the night. This was the paddlewheeler Claudette Durant had wanted him to take to Fargo to protect her from—what?

From whom?

He shook his head. He had no call getting involved. How had she picked him of all the men in St. Louis? He didn't know her or her servant. He didn't even have any clear notion what she wanted from him. For five thousand dollars, though, it had to be dangerous.

Slocum turned to find a saloon, a drink, a game of faro, and maybe a woman. He saw four shadowy forms moving to cut him off from the street. He touched the butt of his pistol and started to draw just as he heard water dripping behind him.

He glanced over his shoulder to see a man rising from the dirty river, a wooden club in his hand. Slocum drew, turned, aimed, and fired in one smooth motion. The man climbing up the piling and onto the dock screeched as the caliber bullet caught him high on the shoulder. He spun around and fell face-first into the Mississippi.

Stars suddenly exploded in Slocum's head. The four men who had been moving up on him slowly had closed the distance too quickly for him to respond. He crashed onto the dock, struggling weakly.

"The son of a bitch went and shot Pete."

A heavy boot caught him in the side and sent pain

lancing throughout his body. He sucked in a lungful of air and screamed. He might have a broken rib. Slocum tried to lift his pistol and fire at his attackers.

Strong hands yanked the six-shooter from his feeble grip. He blinked the sweat from his eyes in time to see the man who had taken his gun flip it around and use the butt to strike out. Pistol-whipped with his own gun!

The butt crashed into his cheek. He felt thick blood spurt from a cut. Another heavy boot found its way to his belly. He gasped and doubled up. As he did so, his fingers sought the derringer in his boot top.

He found it.

Slocum rolled over and fired. The slug caught the man who had been kicking him in the middle of the chest.

Then the world began to move too fast around him. More curses, more orders being barked out. A powerful hand grabbed his wrist and squeezed until the derringer fell from his numb fingers. He tried to kick out, but his legs got tangled in some rope coiled on the dock. Slocum looked up and saw the flash of silver from one attacker's belt. Then everything went away in a cloud of red and black.

The man used Slocum's own pistol to beat him senseless, and when he no longer moved, the man continued his punishment. Soon pain receded as Slocum passed out.

3

John Slocum gasped and sputtered and fought weakly. His arms had turned to lead, and his body throbbed like one giant bruise. Worst of all, he couldn't breathe. Every time he sucked in a lungful of air, pain shot into his chest and consciousness slipped that much further away.

"Quit struggling, damn your eyes!" he heard someone say. He tried to land a right cross on his attacker's chin. A newborn kitten had more punch. But Slocum wasn't going to give in easily.

"He's a feisty one, ain't he?" another voice said.

"Ought to let the stupid son of a bitch drown. Serve him right."

"He surely is dressed fine. Think he's some rich dude who got tangled up over at the Black Dragon?"

"Black Dragon?" Slocum heard a voice croaking, then realized he was trying to speak. "What's that?"

"Got a rise out of him, it did," said the second voice. "That's an opium parlor run by a couple of chinks over on Lincoln Boulevard, not a hundred yards upriver from here. You try smoking a little of the happy-happy tonight, friend?"

"Friend?" Slocum flopped onto his back and stared up into the summer sky. The stars were blurred at first, then sharpened as his vision returned. He coughed and rolled onto his side.

"Go on. Spit up the gallon or two of the Mississippi you swallowed. It'll make you feel better."

"Don't let him puke on the deck, dammit!" flared the first.

Slocum held his supper down. He pulled himself up to his knees, then saw that he was on a barge in the river. It took several more seconds for him to remember what had happened. He had seen the flash of silver on one attacker's belt. Then he had been hit on the head with his own pistol. Slocum cursed as it all came rushing back. They had robbed him, then thrown him into the Mississippi.

His hands worked slowly over his coat and pressed out the muddy river water. As he had expected, the gold coins were gone from his coat pocket. So was the wad of greenbacks. Then he cursed under his breath. Not only had the cutthroats stolen his Colt Navy, they had taken his watch.

That watch was all Slocum had to remember his brother by—except for the sight of the bloody, lifeless body on the battlefield at Gettysburg.

"You ain't been smoking opium, have you? I seen you earlier on tonight in the Lost River Pilot. You're the gambler what took all of Slick's money 'fore Jed throwed you out."

"Seems I played one hand too many," Slocum said. "You two pull me out of the river?"

"We saw you floating face down and thought you was dead. You turned into the liveliest corpse we ever saw, thrashin' and kickin'. I do declare, you'll be a week in your grave before you stop fightin'."

"I sincerely hope so." Slocum stood on shaky legs. His strength returned slowly. "Wish I could reward you men for your good deed, but I seem to have lost everything."

"That's all right," said the second river man. From his tone Slocum knew that they were disappointed.

They probably made good money pulling bodies out of the Mississippi and stripping them. Slocum looked toward the shoreline. The barge fought against the sluggish current and strained a thick hawser fastened to a dock. Slocum figured that the bushwhackers had robbed him and just rolled his body off the dock. He must have floated for several minutes before reaching this bend in the river.

"You might want to remember us later on," said the first. "If you got any money left, that is."

"I'm poor as a churchmouse again," said Slocum. "I got three gents to thank for that." Something in his tone made the two grizzled river men back away.

"You gonna get even with them?"

If he could find them, Slocum would kill them. He asked, "You ever see anyone along the docks wearing a Navajo silver conch belt?"

"Don't reckon I even know what one looks like."

Slocum described the belt and the silver oval links. Neither of the river men admitted to knowing who wore such distinctive jewelry this far from the Southwest Anasazi tribe.

"Thanks again," Slocum said.

"Wait, mister. What you gonna do? We're—"

Slocum didn't wait to hear the rest of the river man's plea to stay. He refused to give them time to think of new devilment. Once, in San Francisco, he had watched crimps working the Embarcadero saloons. They had shanghaied more than twenty men, selling them to sea captains for almost a hundred dollars a head. Slocum didn't think such evil doings went on in St. Louis, but he wasn't going to wait and see.

He knifed into the water with a clean dive. The water almost gagged him again. It was surprisingly warm. He surfaced and gasped for air, then began swimming for the shore through the flotsam that accumulated in the river bend. When he reached shore, he felt completely filthy, body and soul.

He was wet, dirty, weaponless, broke—and madder than hell. He took off his fancy coat and wrung it out. His ruffled white shirt followed. He dried off the rest of his clothes the best he could before dressing again. He didn't look or feel presentable in polite company, but where he was going, it wasn't likely to be any too polite.

He wanted revenge.

Slocum hiked back to the Harbor and Clayton intersection and simply stared at the warehouse where he had met Claudette Durant. Had she sent the bushwackers after him? He thought on it for a few seconds, then decided that Mrs. Durant had been afraid of being discovered. She had no reason to have anyone rob him. She wanted his cooperation in getting to Fargo, not his gold.

Slocum shook his head. From the looks of the pearls and other finery the woman wore so easily, she had more than a band of thieves could accumulate in a year along the river front. However she—or Mr. Durant—made the money, it amounted to a considerable pile.

Slocum decided watching the warehouse did him no good. He had to be more aggressive in finding his Colt and his brother's watch. Slocum figured the gold was gone for good, and he didn't even think about the Yankee greenbacks. Scrip was useless for most transactions that counted.

He looked through the swinging doors in the Lost River Pilot. He saw Jed in the back talking with the owner. Mr. Hicks yawned and motioned Jed away. Slocum saw nothing to hold his interest here. He moved on. The next saloon was two blocks toward the center of St. Louis.

Nothing. And he saw nothing worth mentioning in the next four saloons.

He stood just inside the door of the Gateway Saloon, looking over the small crowd inside. Smoke hung heavily in the air, and the piano player banged out a tune Slocum recognized only after several seconds. He turned to leave when he saw a burly river man at the bar reach across and grab the barkeep by the front of his shirt.

"Gimme another."

"You ain't got enough money to buy a flea another drink, Mattson." The barkeep twisted and pulled free.

Slocum didn't care if the river man had a plugged nickel to his name. When he had reached across the bar, his battered canvas vest had ridden up and revealed an ebony-handled Colt Navy thrust into his belt.

Slocum's Colt.

He slipped out of the Gateway Saloon and watched Mattson through a spot he cleaned off in a dirty windowpane. The man had enough money for another drink. The surprise on the bartender's face convinced Slocum that Mattson was not usually well-heeled.

He knew where the man had come by this night's windfall. Slocum didn't even realize he touched the pocket where his poker winnings had rested. He wanted to go in and grab Mattson by the throat and squeeze until the man disgorged the pistol, the watch, and the money, but Slocum had learned patience. He had been one of the Confederacy's best snipers because he knew how to bide his time and strike only when success was assured. Mattson would give up his secrets soon enough.

Slocum waited for Mattson to run out of money. The man staggered out the front doors of the Gateway Saloon and belched loudly. He scratched himself and squinted at the pink fingers touching the dark night sky. Dawn promised another hot summer St. Louis day in only a few hours.

He stumbled off away from where Slocum stood. On

cat-soft feet, Slocum followed. He wanted to see where Mattson led him. When it became apparent that the man wasn't able to find his way out of a barrel, much less lead him to the others who had robbed him, Slocum acted.

Four quick paces closed the distance. Mattson heard the steps and started to turn, his hand reaching for the Colt shoved into the waist of his britches. Slocum swung with all his strength and landed a fist on the side of the man's head. Mattson lost his balance and tumbled into an alleyway. He tried again to draw the Colt.

Slocum kicked him in the belly. Mattson retched weakly as Slocum recovered his pistol.

"I'll have to clean it," he said in a cold, low voice. "Scum like you touching it might have caused rust."

"What is it, mister?"

Slocum kicked him again to get his attention. "You robbed me a couple hours back." He glanced up and saw the sky lightening with a new day's burning sun. His clothes still clung damply to him. In a very short time, the sun would dry even those soaked rags.

By then, Slocum wanted to know the names of the other two men who had attacked him. He pointed the pistol directly between Mattson's eyes. With deliberate slowness, he cocked the Colt. The first click turned the river man's eyes into wide brown saucers filled with fear. The second click as the hammer came back fully brought forth a babble of denial.

"Shut up, Mattson. All I want to know is who the other two were—especially the dry-gulcher wearing the Navajo conch belt."

"I don't know what you're talking about, mister."

"Goodbye," Slocum said.

Mattson kicked out. The toe of his boot caught Slocum just above the knee. He jerked his shot, sending a bullet digging into the hard dirt beside the river man's head. Slocum grunted with the pain in his leg and started to get the man back in his sights.

Mattson's speed came from desperation. He bowled Slocum over and ran hellbent for leather from the alleyway. Slocum cursed and hobbled after him. The whiskey fog had burned away entirely from Mattson's brain. Fear replaced it

Slocum intended to end that fear as fast as he could. Pushing the pain away, he followed Mattson. The river man ran like the demons of hell nipped at his heels. The way Slocum felt, Mattson would have stood a better chance dickering with them.

Mattson's wits were either addled or he thought Slocum would not be able to follow. He made a beeline directly to a tarpaper shack down by the Mississippi not fifty yards from Clayton Street. Slocum dropped back when the man got to the shack's rickety door. The sun poked up over the horizon and sent golden rays angling across the river. Slocum didn't want to spook the river man again.

Not yet. Not until he made sure the other two bushwhackers weren't inside the shack. Most of all, Slocum wanted the man wearing the Navajo belt. That was the son of a bitch who had pistol-whipped him with his own gun. Deep down inside, Slocum also felt this was the one who had his watch. He looked to be the leader and was most likely to have his pick of the spoils before rolling their victim into the river.

Slocum moved quietly down the muddy bank and dropped to his knees by the shack. He pressed his ear against the rough plank supporting this portion of the shack. Inside he heard Mattson gasping for breath. The frightened retreat from the alley had taken most of the man's wind.

Slocum had just about made up his mind to barge in and question Mattson at great—and most painful— length when he heard a second voice groan.

"Whatsit? What you wantin', Mattson? Can't you let me sleep it off? Got a terrible hangover."

"Willy, we got big trouble."

"You got big trouble if you don't hightail it out of here and let me be."

"No, no, listen. That fellow we dumped into the river."

"What about him?"

Mattson's voice rose in pitch as he explained to Willy. Willy said, "Can't hardly believe no one could have survived. We bashed his head in good."

"It's him, I tell you. He took back the Colt."

"You sure this ain't some drunken hallucination?"

"He wasn't no ghost. He did look like he was drowned, though."

"You knocked him down, then you just upped and came here straight out? God, you got shit for brains. I ought to tie a rock around your scrawny neck and toss you into the Mississippi."

Slocum heard Willy stirring. Clothing rustled as he dressed. Slocum checked his Colt and made sure that he had good loads in it. The way Mattson looked, he might have dropped it in the dirt or the river before sticking it into his belt. The Colt Navy had been finely wrought and even more carefully tended over the years. Slocum was a first rate gunsmith and had lavished great care on the six-shooter.

It was ready.

"We ought to warn—" Mattson was cut off in midsentence.

"He don't want us bothering him. You know how he gets when we can't handle troubles on our own."

"This might go all the way up to—"

"Mattson, shut your face or I'll do it for you. Show me where you left the dude. I'll do what you didn't have the guts to do."

Slocum heard a knife slicing through the air. This squared well with what he had seen of the men. They were more inclined to cut a man's throat when he was unconscious than to face him in a fair fight.

The tarpaper shack trembled as Willy and Mattson emerged. Slocum turned around and, still crouching, took careful aim. The Colt's report sounded like a cannon in the still morning air.

Willy screamed as he fell forward, clutching at his wounded left leg. Mattson stood staring at him, a stupid expression on his face. He turned pale when he looked from his fallen comrade and up into the muzzle of Slocum's six-shooter.

"This makes two of you I've found," Slocum said softly. "Empty your pockets. Both of you. *Now!*"

"I'm hurt. You shot me from behind."

"Willy," Slocum said, "you're lucky I just didn't blow your damned head off. You and Mattson and your boss robbed me last night. I don't take kindly to it."

"We got laws in St. Louis." Mattson licked his lips nervously. Slocum read the man's mind as plainly as if everything had been spelled out on paper.

He thought he and Willy would get a better deal with the local police than with Slocum.

For once Mattson was right. The police weren't likely to shoot him down in cold blood.

Mattson saw blood in Slocum's eye. He began to babble. "We can work this out, mister. Me and Willy. We didn't know what we was doing. He made us do it. Honest."

"Who are you talking about?" Slocum wanted the name.

"Him. You know." Mattson's mouth opened, and then he began sucking air. His arms flailed about. With a single convulsive twitch, he fell forward, face down in the mud. The bullet had caught him squarely in the back of the skull.

Slocum dived onto his belly, his Colt ready to return fire. He saw no one.

"Your boss wants you out of the way real bad. Look at what he did to Mattson," said Slocum. "If you want out of here alive, tell me where my watch is."

"What?" Willy rolled over and stared up the bank and then back at Slocum. "All you care about is the damned watch?"

"You don't have it." Slocum looked through the small pile of debris that Willy had scooped from his pockets. A single gold coin remained. It might have been one stolen off him that night, but Slocum couldn't say. The sight of the gold gleaming in the morning sun startled Willy.

He clutched his wound and sat upright. "Damn, I thought I spent everything last night. Musta got caught in my pocket."

Slocum snared the solitary coin and stuffed it into his shirt pocket. It was little enough to show for his night's misadventure.

Mud fountained beside him as the unseen sniper took another shot. Willy tried to wiggle back to his shack. Slocum kept him covered and said coldly, "Stay put. When you tell me what I want to know, *then* you can get under cover."

"Have a heart, mister," Willy pleaded. A third bullet missed him by inches. Slocum figured the sniper was on top of the Mississippi Shipping offices just down the street from the Lost River Pilot Saloon. Whoever was up there, he was one hell of a good shot and had one fine rifle.

"What's your boss's name?"

"Please!" Willy frantically rolled as another bullet came close to ending his life. Slocum fired and stopped the man from rolling too far away.

"Let him shoot you or let me. It doesn't much matter."

"You wouldn't just up and walk off. I see it in your eyes. You're gonna kill me."

"Probably. But there's a small chance. With him—" Slocum indicated the distant sniper—"you have no chance at all."

"I don't have the watch. I gave it to a whore."

"Which one?" Slocum's patience wore thin. He ducked when the sniper put a round through the tarpaper shack and narrowly missed his head. Slocum reckoned the man must be using a Sharps .69 to get such accuracy at this range. The hole left in the tarpaper supported his speculation on the matter.

"Hell, mister, how should I know? She had red hair. Smallish, but with a great—" Slocum shot Willy in the other leg.

"I don't care about such things. Where is she?"

"Enid! That's it. Her name is Enid, over at the Wagons West Casino."

"You're doing better. What's the name of..." Slocum's voice trailed off. The sniper had finally found Willy's range. The heavy lead slug drove down through the man's shoulder, smashing bone and ripping into his heart.

Slocum stared into the sun and tried to make out the sniper. He couldn't. He heaved a sigh and thrust his Colt into its holster. Two of the men were dead—and both at the hands of their partner.

Slocum didn't have much to go on but the whore's name. One thing was for sure. He would get back his brother's watch.

4

John Slocum returned to his hotel room and ignored the stares he got from the desk clerk and the two men sitting in the drawing room reading the newspaper. He knew he looked like a drowned river rat and he didn't much care. He had been through too much in the past few hours to care about the opinions of others.

He stripped off his fancy clothing and rummaged through his belongings. The only other clothes he had were for the trail. For the work that lay ahead, rougher denims and a cotton shirt would suffice. He needed a bath but didn't want to take the time. The quick dip in the muddy Mississippi would have to hold him—although that had produced most of the filth that clung so tenaciously to him.

One thing he did take the time to check and clean was his Colt Navy. The precision pistol had to work properly or he might find himself holding a lump of worthless metal when he needed it the most. He stripped the six-shooter and carefully scrubbed the blued metal until he was sure it worked to perfection. He spent another five minutes loading it. A misfire might mean more than losing his brother's watch.

It could mean death.

Slocum turned cold inside when he thought about the sniper who had killed Mattson and Willy. He faced one hell of a good marksman—possibly as good as he was himself. The only thing he knew about the man, other than his sharpshooting ability, was that he wore a silver conch belt.

Slocum oiled down the inside of his soft leather holster and settled it into place on his left side. He made a few practice draws, reaching across his body and swiftly bringing the Colt to bear on his reflection in the mirror. The plunge into the river hadn't damaged the holster. Slocum winced as he moved, though. The beating had left him aching and bruised.

He settled his hat on his head and then left the hotel. He didn't want to face the room clerk again and tell him payment might be delayed. He slipped out the back way, down an alley and into the streets of St. Louis.

Morning had brought with it incredible activity. If the city lacked much in the way of entertainment after dark, the people made up for it with their industry during the daylight hours. The dock area swarmed with agents and representatives from the shipping companies. All sought transportation up and down the mighty river.

Slocum paused as he passed by the berthed *Pride of Orleans*. This was the riverboat Claudette Durant had been so insistent that they take to Fargo. He studied the boat more carefully. Most of the larger paddlewheelers had a draft of over six feet. He guessed this boat drew less than half that, making it ideal for travelling the shallower tributaries on the upper Minnesota River. What drew the woman to this particular vessel, Slocum couldn't say.

For that matter, why she wanted to go to a godforsaken place like Fargo was beyond all knowing.

He walked quickly past the office of the Mississippi Shipping Company. The sniper had few other choices for his firing tripod than the roof of this building. Slocum glanced over his shoulder. It lay in a straight line with Willy's tarpaper shack.

Slocum decided he could look into the matter later— after he had talked to a woman named Enid at the

SLOCUM AND THE RED RIVER RENEGADES 35

Wagons West Casino. It took him twenty minutes to find the tumbled-down saloon. He patted his pockets and found only the single gold coin he had taken back from Willy. Still, twenty dollars was more than he'd had in his pocket all winter long.

He went into the dim, smoky room. A simple plank balanced across three crates formed the bar. The mirror behind the barkeep had been broken at some time in the past and badly repaired. Many pieces were completely missing. Two drunks lay passed out on tables in the back, and a gin rummy game played itself out at a table in the front.

Slocum looked over the card players. The eight pennies on the table looked to be their entire poke.

"What'll you have, mister?" asked the bartender.

"Beer," Slocum said, not daring to try the whiskey. In a dive like this, all he could expect would be trade whiskey. He didn't want to poison himself with the cheap alcohol, gunpowder, nitric acid, and rusty nails they usually tossed into such a concoction.

The weak brew set in front of him confirmed his suspicions. This wasn't the place to do serious drinking.

"You look like you're in need of some ... female company," the barkeep said.

Slocum didn't try to hold back the slow grin that spread on his face. The bartender had saved him from asking.

"I see that the idea suits you just fine," the barkeep said. "We got a couple girls upstairs in the cribs right now. Either of 'em would tickle your fancy, unless I miss my guess."

"I'm partial to redheads," he said. "Not too big, either. Small-like."

"We got one here that answers to that description," the barkeep said, "but she ain't on duty right now. How about one with dark hair? And not so small?"

"As long as she's female," Slocum said, not wanting to make the man suspicious.

"Bertha is a real man-pleaser. Upstairs and first door on the left. Knock and go on in."

Slocum turned and felt the barkeep's hand on his arm. "That's ten dollars for the whore and another two bits for the beer."

Slocum dropped the double eagle on the stained warped planking. The barkeep scooped it up on the first bounce. He slapped the change down. Slocum retrieved it, not wanting to make a scene. All he wanted right now was to find Enid and his watch.

As Slocum started up the creaking stairs to the second-floor cribs, he saw the barkeep take his untouched beer and pour it back into the barrel.

At the head of the stairs, he found Bertha's door, but he wasn't interested in her. He walked slowly down the narrow corridor and stopped in front of a dilapidated door with the name Enid crudely carved into it. A quick glance around showed no one watching.

He tried the door. The knob came off in his hand. He thrust it back on and leaned against the door panel. With a protesting sigh, the door creaked open.

Slocum was ready for anything. He expected to find Enid sprawled on the bed, maybe with a man. The dingy room was empty. A ray of sunlight slanted in through a dirty window and fell across the unmade bed.

The bright sunbeam stopped on a trunk, just like a rainbow pointed to a pot of gold at its end. Slocum closed the door and went to the trunk. He started rummaging through it, hoping to find his watch. All he found were women's clothes, mostly unwashed, and Enid's few pitiful keepsakes.

Slocum looked under the bed and found nothing but dirt and items he failed to identify—but he knew they weren't his watch.

"What'n bloody 'ell's going on 'ere?" a loud voice cried.

Slocum swung around, his knees grating into the splintery floorboards. Towering over him stood a bull of a man—and one he recognized instantly.

The silver conch belt gleamed in the sunlight coming through the window.

Slocum started for his pistol. Even as he began the draw, he knew he wouldn't make it. The man took one step forward and launched a kick intended to crush Slocum's head. Slocum managed to twist to one side. The glancing blow drove him into the bed and made it impossible to draw his pistol.

"You bleedin' son of a bitch. You're the one from last night!"

The man drew a thick-bladed knife and slashed at Slocum's face. The hot edge passed by his cheek. Slocum knew he had been cut from the rush of blood, but he paid it no heed. To have done so would have meant death.

He got one leg free and swept it around like a scythe. He tangled himself between the other man's legs and brought him crashing to the ground.

"You bleedin' barstid! I'll kill you for this!"

The man with the Navajo conch belt struggled to get his feet back under him. Slocum rose first and whipped out his six-shooter.

"Don't try it." The click of the Colt's hammer coming back emphasized the command.

"You stupid git," the river man grumbled. He drove his knife into the floor and backed off.

Slocum got a better chance to study the man. From his accent he was British. His clothing placed him firmly as a river man. His powerful hands and trunklike torso betrayed a strength that Slocum didn't want to oppose head-on.

"The watch," he said. The man read death in Slocum's eyes.

The Britisher cocked his head to one side, then said, "That's what you want, mate? The bleedin' *watch?*"

"The watch," Slocum repeated.

"You'd kill a man over a hunk of tin that don't even keep good time?"

"Yes." Slocum didn't bother going down the list of other reasons he'd be happy to empty all six shots into the river man's gut.

"You're a strange one."

"I don't like having what's mine stolen. Where is the watch?"

"Willy gave it to the whore who lives here."

"Enid."

The man's bushy eyebrows rose in double arches as he looked down on Slocum's six-foot frame. "You do get around, don't you? Next time, we're gonna have to make sure you don't crawl back out of the river."

Something in the man's manner caused Slocum to turn wary. The river man bellowed out his words. Through the thunder of his bull-throated speech Slocum heard the clicking of boot heels in the hallway. He dropped to one knee and fired just as another river man swung a cargo hook. The pistol's report echoed painfully in the tiny room, and the cloud from the black powder filled the air.

Slocum let the river man fall past him. The hook stuck into the floor, but this wasn't the vibration Slocum felt. The Britisher in the silver conch belt had pried loose his knife and now brandished it.

Slocum fired in his direction. He knew he had missed when the huge river man kept coming. Slocum rolled past the sailor he had shot and crashed into the corridor. Women shrieked from several of the rooms. Half-dressed men peered out of two doorways. Coming up the stairs, the barkeep and three others blocked escape, armed and ready for a fight.

Slocum fired again—and again he missed the Britisher. He was lucky to escape with his hide intact. The river man's heavy knife had cartwheeled through the air and buried itself hilt-deep in the wall beside Slocum's head.

Getting his feet under him, Slocum plunged down the hall and toward a broken window. Angry cries behind gave him extra speed. He dived through the window. Glass splintered and cut him. He had only a brief instant to react when he saw where he was falling. Slocum tucked in his head and tried to somersault. He crashed in a heap of garbage tossed out of the casino and the restaurant next door.

"There the bloke is. Stop 'im and I'll see you get a fiver!" The Brit waved his huge fist at Slocum.

He looked up and tried to bring his six-shooter onto target. Before he could, the river man ducked back inside the casino.

Slocum knew better than to wait. He got up and brushed off the biggest chunks of the garbage, then ran as hard as he could for the end of the alley. He spun into the street and slowed his pace. Not fifty feet away patrolled a pair of St. Louis police. Their blue uniforms and brass buttons marked them, even if the long night sticks they swung easily by leather thongs hadn't.

Slocum never once considered approaching them. If the police here were anything like those in other "civilized" cities, they were paid off by the political bosses. Slocum had no idea who owned the Wagons West Casino. From the number of men swarming in when he raised the ruckus in Enid's room, he might find himself in worse trouble than ever.

Besides, this was his quarrel. He didn't want the law involved. All he wanted now was to get his watch back and to get the hell out of St. Louis.

He drew a few curious stares as he walked along the street reeking of garbage. Slocum stopped and ducked down a side street when he thought he saw two men following him. An empty doorway gave the chance he needed. He slipped into it, his back against the cold door. Hand on pistol, he waited.

The two men hurried by, passed, and then stopped. One scratched his head. The other said, "We done lost him. Zeb's gonna be madder'n hell over this."

"*I'm* madder'n hell," the other said. "He promised us five dollars each if we caught him. Where else can we make easy money?"

"Zebediah Matthews ain't the sort to go throwing his money around, neither," agreed the first.

Slocum smiled. He knew the man's name now. Getting the watch back might be as easy as asking Enid for it—or as hard as killing Matthews. At the moment, Slocum was tired and aching, and he didn't much care what he had to do to get his property back.

He let the two men go on. He doubled back to the Wagons West. The saloon had a few more customers than before, but not many. It was only seven in the morning. The gambling wouldn't start until sundown. Slocum snorted. And in St. Lous, it wouldn't last longer than midnight.

He pushed all that from his mind when he heard a woman's shrill cry. He looked into the saloon and saw a red-haired woman on the stairs leading up to the cribs. Standing three steps below her and still looking her in the eye was Zebediah Matthews. He grabbed her by the hair and shook her until the woman's teeth rattled. Slocum checked himself. He didn't want to rush in and find himself staring down the barrel of a shotgun.

The barkeep watched the argument with bored indifference. Slocum didn't doubt the man had seen this a hundred times before.

"You stupid tart!" bellowed Matthews. "You know 'im. You must! How else did 'e find this place?"

"Zeb, please," she moaned. "I don't know. I don't. You're hurting me!"

"I'll hurt you a mite more unless you tell me who 'e is."

"He . . . he's just another customer. I don't know. Zebediah, please!" The burly river man jerked at the woman's hair. For a sickening instant, Slocum thought Matthews had ripped out a handful of the rusty-red hair. The woman fell back on the stairs. Matthews towered above her.

"Get up to your room, you silly cow. I'll talk to you more in a few minutes." As Matthews turned, Slocum saw the watch chain dangling from the man's pants pocket just under the conch belt. Matthews had had the watch all the time.

Slocum drew his pistol and went directly into the saloon. "Move and I'll blow your head off," he called to Matthews. The giant river man froze on the stairs, his face a mask of rage.

"I thought I was done with you, mate. Seems you keep turnin' up like a bad penny." Matthews motioned to the barkeep.

Slocum never hesitated. He swung around, fired, then returned to cover Matthews. His slug had caught the barkeep in the shoulder and spun him around. The man lay behind the bar sobbing in pain. But Matthews had vanished in that brief instant.

Slocum cursed. The British river man was built like Goliath and moved faster than a striking rattler. He ran across the large room and started up the stairs when he heard voices outside.

"That's the man, officer. You arrest him and you'll be amply rewarded."

Slocum didn't see who spoke, but he did see the three policemen shoving past the swinging doors and into the Wagons West. At the head of the stairs Zeb Matthews waited for him. The fight to regain his watch would be titanic against that muscular river man.

Slocum couldn't get back his brother's watch before having his head bashed in by the club-swinging police. A second look at the three advancing on him convinced him to run. One fumbled for a pistol under his long blue jacket. If they unlimbered their six-shooters and began firing, he would never leave the saloon alive.

Slocum kicked and caught one policeman in the belly. The man dropped his club and stumbled back into the second. The third stepped to the side and aimed.

Slocum fired blindly. His shot filled the air between them with obscuring smoke. He heard the policeman's bullet wing by just inches over his head. He ducked and got into the back room. From there, he dashed into the alley and past the pile of garbage that had broken his fall earlier. No matter what he did, he couldn't get away from that stinking compost heap.

John Slocum had failed. For the moment. But he would be back. He knew what Matthews looked like—and he knew the man had his watch.

5

Slocum sat by the river, washing off the worst of the filth covering him. The Mississippi's muddy water was hardly better than what he peeled off, but the water helped cool him. The sun had risen high in the cloudless sky and scorched the city. He lay back and stared up into the azure sky and waited for the first signs of puffy white clouds to appear. Almost an hour after Slocum started waiting, the clouds built up in the west.

"A thunderstorm," he said to himself, seeing the anvil shapes and the dark underbellies. "Cool everything off a mite."

He lay back down and closed his eyes. Nothing had gone right for him in the past ten months. The trapping in the Wasatch Mountains had been a disaster. Coming to St. Louis and gambling had paid off—for a time. Last night his luck had turned sour again.

Without even realizing it, Slocum's hand drifted to his watch pocket and rubbed over the empty slot.

He propped his head up on an elbow and considered ways of recovering his stolen property. From all he had seen, Zebediah Matthews was one tough hombre. That didn't scare Slocum. He had come out on top of better men than Matthews. What did give him pause was how to get back the watch.

He didn't want Matthews destroying it out of spite. Plans formed and were discarded as Slocum sat and watched the Mississippi River traffic. A half dozen sternwheelers paddled by sedately, as if they didn't have a care in the world. For those aboard the fabulous riverboats, they might not have a care. Slocum did.

Without consciously knowing it, he came to a conclusion and a plan formed in his head. The man seemed to be known around the Wagons West Casino. In spite of him being so obviously a river man, he might have some interest in the saloon.

Slocum had seen similar arrangements before. In return for keeping the peace in the saloon when he was in town, Matthews might receive a share of the profits. Or he might have bought into the saloon. Or—and this seemed more likely to Slocum—perhaps Zebediah Matthews was the pimp who watched out for the whores and their money.

All he had to do was waylay the man. No need to get fancy about it. Slocum had robbed enough men in his day to do it right.

Those memories rose and filled his mouth with bile. He had done his share of killing and stealing, but usually for what he thought a good cause. Matthews and his two henchmen had robbed him just to take his money and spend it on whores.

Slocum walked past the hotel where he had stayed during his better-off days in St. Louis. He had two bits less than ten dollars now instead of damned near a thousand dollars. He shrugged off the notion of leaving what tack he had in the hotel room. It was a small enough price to pay for the week he spent there. What he had on his back was enough to get him by.

He went into the restaurant next to the Wagons West and sat at a table affording him a good view of the street and those in it. He ordered a beefsteak, fried potatoes, and a cup of coffee to wash it down. When he finished, he felt better than he had in twenty-four hours.

"Here," he said, giving the waiter three dollars. "Keep the change." It made little difference to him if he had ten dollars or five in his pocket—or none at all. Living by his wits had got him by before. It would continue to be enough.

While he was eating he had seen a steady stream of men entering and leaving the Wagons West, but none had been Matthews. Slocum circled the saloon and tried to figure out if he might have missed the man. The back door was barred on the inside. This told him nothing.

Slocum shrugged it off. The only way of finding out what he really needed to know was to grab the bull by the horns. He returned to the boardwalk and hesitated for a moment in the doorway of the saloon. Then he pushed inside.

He tensed, waiting for the hue and cry to go up. He relaxed a mite when he saw that a different barkeep worked behind the wood planking. Two bouncers lounged near the stairs leading to the cribs, but he did not recognize either of them, and they weren't likely to place him for a hurried description.

Slocum sat down at a table and dropped what coins he had on the table. "Deal me in," he told the man shuffling. Nobody paid him mind.

Slocum played blackjack for almost an hour and won consistently. His winnings were not enough to draw attention, but he had almost fifty dollars in scrip stacked in front of him when Enid strutted in. She stood in the doorway and surveyed the crowd, one hand on her jutting hip.

"Now that's my kind of woman," Slocum said. He scooped up his money, and nobody said a word. The dealer simply passed over his spot at the table as he dealt out a new round of blackjack.

"Howdy, mister," Enid said when he walked over, rolling her hips seductively. "You looking for some... fun?"

"I reckon you can supply all the fun I can stand," Slocum said. She had a black eye and had done a poor job of covering it with thick makeup. From the way she held her left arm, he guessed that she might have bruises where Matthews had grabbed her earlier on.

"That I can—and I'm reasonable."

"Let's go upstairs and talk about it."

"Talk? Is that all you want?" She winked lewdly and linked her arm with his. They passed the two guards at the bottom of the stairs. Neither of the men paid Slocum the slightest attention. He was just another customer going to the cribs for a quick tumble.

Slocum led the way and stopped in front of Enid's room. Her eyebrows rose. "How did you know this was my room?" she asked suspiciously. "You ain't been with me before. I'd've remembered a man like you. I surely would have." She ran her fingers up and down his arms, feeling the play of muscles there.

Slocum pushed into the room. The bed hadn't been made and the mess left by the fight with Matthews still littered the floor. Housekeeping obviously wasn't Enid's long suit.

Even the time he took giving the room such a cursory examination had given Enid time to begin undressing. She shrugged her thin shoulders and worked the dress down to reveal her breasts. Slocum found himself admiring them. They weren't big; they were hardly larger than apples. But, like apples, they were firm and looked tasty.

"Don't just look. You can touch."

"I want Zebediah Matthews."

"What?" Enid stopped and stared at him. A look of slow horror replaced the false lust. "No, you aren't the one who was in here last night. You can't be. Zeb said he done you good, that you'd never be back."

"I saw what he did to you this morning." Slocum reached out and gently touched the dark bruises on her arm. She pulled back.

"That's none of your concern."

"It is, though," he said. "Matthews beat you up because of me."

The red-haired woman tipped her head to one side and stared at him in amazement. "You really *do* care, don't you?"

"Where's Matthews?"

"He'll kill you, mister. He's one mean son of a bitch."

"I want him. Tell me where he is, and you won't have to worry about him beating you up any more."

Enid smiled almost shyly. "There's a price for the information."

Slocum reached into the pocket of his denims to pull out the money he had just won at the blackjack game. Enid crossed the small room and put her hand on his. "No," she said softly. "That's not the price."

Slocum saw flashes of her desperation, her despair. He bent over and kissed her on the lips. She backed away and sat on the edge of the bed.

"Please. I . . . I want to feel like a real woman again. Not some whore who has to give everything to Zeb Matthews. You make me think you really respect me for a woman."

Slocum went over and put his hand on her cheek. She turned and kissed his hand, turned it over and kissed the palm. Her tongue snaked out and left a tiny wet spot. She worked down the fingers and kissed every fingertip. With her free hand she drew him closer.

Slocum swung around and sat beside her on the bed. Her dress fell to her waist, her firm breasts pressing close against him. She threw her arms around his neck and kissed him with a fervor that took his breath away.

He hadn't intended getting involved with her. He had wanted information about Matthews and nothing more. But he felt himself responding to her obvious need, and he surprised himself when he realized desires boiled in his own loins.

His hands slipped around Enid's bare back and down her spine. She lifted herself off the bed enough for him to finish skinning her out of the thin dress she wore. The woman lay back on the bed, her milky thighs opening to reveal a ruddy patch between her legs. She was no rich city beauty, but she had a dignity about her that Slocum couldn't deny.

He let her unbutton his shirt. He followed it with his gunbelt, boots, and trousers.

"Do whatever you want," Enid whispered hotly in his ear. "I . . . I want you."

She had said that to hundreds of men, Slocum knew. But she sounded as if she meant it. And she might. Slocum silenced her by pressing his lips against hers, then working down the jut of her jaw to the hollow under her ear. She moaned and arched on the bed as he tongued her earlobe. He kissed and bit gently and then pioneered a pathway even lower.

He came to twin peaks of her firm breasts. His tongue slithered up the left breast and teased the rosy nipple. Sucking it into his mouth, he used tongue and teeth to make the woman moan even louder.

"Oh, I knew it. God, you're so good. Do it more. Please!"

He abandoned her left breast in favor of her right. He saw no reason to give one the full treatment and ignore the other. By the time both nipples stood upright like pointing fingers and he felt the throb of her heart through them, Enid was ready for him.

Her legs drifted apart even more, and she pulled him atop her. "Now, please, but go slow. Zeb always hurried. Don't hurry. Please."

Her plaintive pleading made Slocum check his own rampaging emotions. He positioned himself carefully. She reached down and touched his hot shaft. She stroked along its turgid length, then tugged him toward her most intimate regions.

Enid sobbed out incoherently as he moved forward slightly. He felt himself surrounded by hot, clinging female flesh. Sinking inward slowly caused Enid to arch her back even more.

"Do it," she whimpered. "Take me hard!"

Slocum didn't listen to this. He moved with great deliberation, keeping himself under strict control to give her as much enjoyment as she had ever received. His back-and-forth movements were slow and built Enid's passions.

Her legs circled his waist and locked firmly behind his back. He was trapped now and wouldn't easily escape her. And he found himself not wanting to. Slocum bent forward and licked at the woman's nipples. Her desires had burned unabated in her body before. And they turned into a raging forest fire.

"Yes, no, oh, yes, yes!" Enid's entire body shivered like a leaf caught in a high wind. Slocum saw a red flush rising on her shoulders and neck and knew she was close.

His powerful hips worked even faster. The two of them slowly ceased being man and woman and became one. Slocum was aware of Enid crying out and then sagging weakly just seconds before the hot tide rose within him and exploded outward.

He kept pumping for another minute until he felt himself turning flaccid. Slocum slumped and rested his head beside hers. Red hair fell into his eyes. He rolled off the woman and brushed her hair away.

She turned to him and snuggled close. "This is just like having a real man," she said.

"Thanks a lot."

"That's not what I meant. Not like that. I never enjoyed it like this. Not before." In a lower voice, she added, "Not since Jacob, a long time ago."

Slocum knew she had exposed a part of her past—and soul—to him. He didn't want to pry.

Enid moved even closer, one hand on his chest and her mouth at his ear. She kissed and nibbled his earlobe as he had done to her earlier. He started to push away when she whispered, "Zeb's gone north. He ain't in St. Louis and won't be back for a month or more."

"Where'd he go?" Slocum asked, more sharply than he had intended. Enid moved away, the mood broken.

"You surely do want him in a bad way, don't you?" She read the answer in Slocum's eyes. Enid heaved a big sigh and swung her legs off the bed. She picked up her dress and climbed into it. "Here's your clothes." She tossed his trousers and shirt to him.

Slocum dressed quickly. He got his boots on and felt completely dressed when he settled his gunbelt around his waist.

"Zebediah's gone north," she repeated. "He shipped out on a steamboat bound for the Red River haul."

"The Red River?"

"He's going on up the river and across to Fargo. Him and his boss have business up there. I never asked what."

"Fargo," mused Slocum. He shook his head. It never failed that events came in lumps. Claudette Durant had wanted him to accompany her to Fargo. Now he found out that Zebediah Matthews and his watch were on the way upriver.

"He'll be back," Enid said with a shudder. "He always is."

"Don't expect him this time," Slocum said. He reached into his denims again for money. Enid again stopped him.

"Please, no. Let me pretend we did it because you

wanted me, and I wanted you, and that there wasn't no money involved."

Slocum bent and kissed her one last time, then spun and left. He had a man to find, and he knew where to look for him now.

6

John Slocum kept fingering the money in his pocket. He had not won enough to do much good. A hundred dollars seemed like a king's ransom when he had nothing. Now that he had lost ten times that—more!—it burned a hole in his pocket.

For all the wealth he started with, Slocum rapidly spent it on bribes finding out about Zebediah Matthews. And what he found out made his blood boil.

He had missed Matthews by a hair. While he had been taking a tumble in the hay with Enid, the burly English river man had been on a steamboat leaving St. Louis. The best Slocum could tell, Matthews had been gone almost six hours. That put him fifty miles or more upriver and out of Slocum's reach.

For the moment.

He wasn't going to let Matthews get away with anything. Not if he had to follow him to the ends of the earth.

He had to spend even more of his remaining gambling winnings to make certain that Matthews *had* been aboard the *Mississippi Princess*. The ugly thought had come to him that Enid might be in cahoots with Matthews, that her fear of him exceeded good sense. Slocum found it hard to believe the woman had faked the passion they had shared, but he wasn't above thinking on it some. When he had only five dollars left, he had found no fewer than four men lounging about the dock area who had seen—and heard—Zeb Matthews bellowing aboard the departing paddlewheeler. One had even claimed to see the man on the foredeck telling longshoremen where to store bales of supplies bound upriver.

Slocum didn't know how much of what Enid had told him was a lie. He did know she'd been truthful about Matthews going to Fargo.

He shook his head in wonderment. What lay in Fargo that drew people like a magnet? Claudette Durant had wanted to go there, too.

Slocum went to the docks, found a ticketing agent, and began asking about boats leaving for Fargo. A sleepy-eyed agent looked up at him, yawned, and said, "You can't go there from here. Not straightaways, at any rate. You got to go up the Mississippi, get to the Minnesota River, then port over to the Red River and on up to Fargo. That's quite a ways to go unless you got some burnin' business there."

The clerk cocked his head to one side and lifted an eyelid further to take in Slocum. The clerk snorted. "Can't see as where you've got any business a'tall goin' up there."

"Would it be easier to buy a horse and ride?" Slocum asked.

"Nope. Boat's fastest, even with having to port over. Heard tell that Mr. Hill's got one right fine spur line running from the Minnesota over to the Red."

Slocum nodded. He had also heard that the Canadian railroad magnate had finished building the last of the bridges needed for the Great Northern to go all the way West. The railroad builder had almost gone bankrupt several times because he, unlike the Northern Pacific Railroad, hadn't accepted any government subsidies for his work. Slocum didn't have much truck with any of the railroad men, but Hill had gumption.

It also looked as if Hill's railroad might provide

needed transportation once he got to Dakota Territory—
if Matthews's destination was really Fargo.

"How much to get up the Minnesota to this railhead?" he asked.

"More'n you got, unless I miss it by a country mile," the clerk said. "We charge the standard. Six cents a mile for passengers, a nickel a pound for freight up the Missouri all the way to Bismarck. But you ain't wanting to go that way, are you?"

"How much to the Great Northern railhead?" Slocum repeated.

The clerk's eyelids drooped. "Fifty-four dollars even gets you berth on the cargo deck. An extra dollar a day and the Mississippi Shipping Company, in its infinite charity, will feed you. You wouldn't be wantin' rates quoted on a *stateroom,* now would you?" The clerk closed both eyes when he saw Slocum's expression. "Didn't think so."

Slocum had spent too much learning of Matthews's plans. The five dollars would feed him, but it wouldn't get him on the man's trail in style—or at all. He could hardly hope to find ammunition for five dollars, much less a horse and tack. Thoughts of stealing a horse and heading cross-country rose in his mind. He pushed them away.

He wasn't out on the frontier where he might stand a chance of getting away. A posse following him would have no trouble learning from the hundreds of settlers to the west of St. Louis where he had gone.

Slocum eyed the broad, muddy expanse of the Mississippi and decided against horse theft. He'd have to ferry over. Escaping would be impossible if they decided to make an example of him.

"We hang horse thieves in St. Louis," the clerk said. Slocum jumped. He had thought the man had fallen asleep.

Slocum turned and walked off, wondering how far a

SLOCUM AND THE RED RIVER RENEGADES 55

stake of five dollars would get him in a poker game. Not far. He'd have to start with penny-ante and work up to a big game. He heaved a deep sigh. He had been too eager to get on Matthews's trail. He should have conserved his money.

Walking to the edge of the dock, he watched the loading of the *Pride of Orleans*. The boat had dropped only a foot in the water, yet her decks were now fully stowed with boxes bound for the north. He leaned against a piling and tried to judge his chances of stowing away. He had heard the stories of riverboat captains and what they did to stowaways. The best he could hope for was geting his ears cut off.

The worst was a hell of a long swim with his hands tied behind his back and a length of iron bar bent around his legs.

A half dozen river men stood on the gangway guarding the cargo. As he watched, Slocum saw one guard grab an urchin and toss him into the river. The boy had tried to sneak aboard, probably to see what he could rob from the staterooms.

"Matthews is going upriver," he said to himself. "I've got to get going, too. How?"

Giving him the answer to his question, Claudette Durant came bustling down the dock and went directly to the biggest of the river men on the gangplank. Slocum couldn't hear what she said, but the man kept shaking his head. When he crossed his thick arms over a barrel chest, Slocum knew the woman had lost her argument.

She stamped her foot and turned away. Slocum had no desire to nursemaid the woman on her journey, but fate had cast them together. He needed her money now, and she was headed in the same direction, for whatever reason. They needed one another, and Slocum wasn't about to pass up this chance.

"Pardon, Mrs. Durant." He tipped his hat. Slocum

was aware of the dust cloud this formed. It had been a spell since he'd had a chance to take a good bath and he had been through hell backwards in the past few days. "Couldn't help noticing he was giving you some trouble. Anything I can do to help out?"

"Mr. Slocum," she said, her nose tipping upward in disdain. "We have had this conversation already. You have spurned my offer of employment."

"Maybe things have changed. If the job is still open, maybe I'm more amenable now."

Claudette Durant looked back over her shoulder at the man standing on the dock, his arms still crossed over his immense chest.

"The offer is still open, sir."

"See you all the way to Fargo?"

"Yes."

"What else is there to this, Mrs. Durant?" Slocum knew there had to be a hidden trap. She had proposed too much money before unless something was badly wrong.

"There is no need to go into the matter more fully," she said, her voice cold. Slocum noticed that her cheeks colored and more than a hint of a French accent came into her words.

"Can't see myself getting those boys riled up unless I hear more about it," said Slocum. The roustabouts had gathered in a tight knot. The giant of a man in the center pointed at Slocum.

"My luggage is aboard the *Pride of Orleans*. I had it smuggled on in packing crates with other names stencilled on the outside."

"Clever," Slocum said. "Why do you want to go to Fargo so bad?"

Claudette Durant fixed her pale gray eyes on his green ones. A small breeze blew across the river and mussed her flawlessly coiffured blonde hair. Slocum thought this insignificant change made Claudette Durant all the more beautiful. It showed she wasn't the perfect lady and made her seem almost human. Almost.

"I want a divorce," she said.

Slocum blinked and looked at her. She returned his gaze steadily. She meant what she said.

"I don't understand. Why not get one in St. Louis?"

"No, you do not understand. My husband is able to keep the matter before the courts for many, many months here. In Fargo the divorce, for a price, can be granted in one day."

Slocum scratched his head. He remembered hearing something about this a few years back but he hadn't paid it any heed.

"So you want a divorce in a hurry?"

"As soon as possible. We must first get aboard the *Pride of Orleans*. It steams from this port in only one hour."

"That sissy servant of yours going along?"

"Pierre remains in St. Louis," Mrs. Durant said testily. "He is loyal to me but wants nothing to do with crossing my husband."

"Reckon a man could get riled finding out a trusted servant helped his wife get a divorce, and he didn't know squat about it. Is Mr. Durant in these parts?"

"His offices are down the street. Where my husband is at the moment is no concern of yours. And, frankly, I could not care less." Claudette Durant sniffed and stuck her nose into the air again. "He's probably with some cheap soiled dove. He prefers their company to mine."

"Then the man's a fool," said Slocum, meaning it. Claudette Durant was a fine looking woman.

Mrs. Durant eyed him again. Slocum saw no friendliness in her. "Will you help me? I can pay five hundred dollars."

"You offered five thousand before."

"My predicament has worsened. My husband has

seen fit to wire the bank and cut off my household allowance. I am unable to offer more."

Even five hundred dollars was a princely sum. He wondered at her generosity. Getting aboard the steamboat wouldn't be that hard. Her husband must have a longer reach than it appeared.

"He doesn't want you leaving St. Louis, does he?"

"Of course not. Benjamin is very possessive. Now, sir, will you aid me, or must I look elsewhere?"

He couldn't deny that Lady Luck had tossed him a hatful of good fortune. Slocum didn't see how acting as bodyguard would be that difficult. He glanced over his shoulder at the roustabouts. Their bulk exceeded their brains. Best of all this trip gave him the chance to track down Zebediah in Fargo.

"Consider it done," he said. Slocum paused when he saw the expression flickering across Mrs. Durant's stony face. He had missed something. "What aren't you telling me?" he asked.

"My daughter is accompanying us."

He shrugged. Two instead of one. This couldn't be any worse.

"Her belongings already on board?" he asked.

"They are, sir. The steamboat leaves in forty-five minutes. How do you intend to get me on?"

Slocum rubbed his chin as he thought. "Give me fifty dollars of the pay and meet me upriver about a half mile as soon as you can. There's a rickety pier there, if memory serves."

Mrs. Durant paused, obviously not trusting him. Then she fumbled in her clutch purse and drew out five crisp ten-dollar greenbacks and passed them to him without a word. He nodded and started off. He had work to do if they were to get away on time.

The roustabouts watched Mrs. Durant rather than him. Slocum held back to see if any of the river men followed her. None did. Satisfied that she and her daughter could reach the pier without his help, Slocum went downriver a ways until he found the two men who had pulled him out of the Mississippi. They lounged on a dock, spat into the river, and whittled as they watched the boats steaming along.

"Lookee here," said the first one. "Our drowned rat has come back."

"I told you boys I'd repay you for what you did, when I could." Slocum pulled out one of the crisp ten-dollar bills Mrs. Durant had given him. "You willing to earn this?"

"Who we got to kill?" spoke up the second.

"Now hold on there, Petey. What you want us to do, mister?"

"You got a boat?"

"Can't say as we have," said Petey. "Stole the one we picked you up in the last night."

"Hush up." The other man stuck his knife in the wood planking and spat. The thick gobbet whirled and twisted on the river's sluggish currents before vanishing under the pier. "We can get another boat, but it'll cost you." The gleam in his eyes told how much.

Slocum heaved a sigh as if exasperated. "Of course you'll have to *rent* one," he said, lying through his teeth. He knew how they would get their boat—and he didn't care.

"Another ten?" asked the leader of the pair.

"Seems fair," allowed Slocum.

"When you want the boat and where we got to take you?"

"There'll be three of us. The pier upriver just past the bend."

"Proctor Point. We know the place like the backs of our hands." Petey held up a gnarled hand and stared at it, as if for the first time.

"Get there as quick as you can. You're going to ferry us out to the middle of the river."

"You wantin' to get on a steamboat without goin' up the gangway, is that it?"

"You do this often?" Slocum asked.

"Often enough, though we usually don't do it in daylight."

Slocum laughed. He had fallen in with a pair of smugglers. He hurried off to get what he could from his room. If he paid the two river men twenty for their trouble, that left him thirty to square accounts at the hotel.

The clerk wrinkled his nose when Slocum came in. "Want to pay up and get on the trail," he told the clerk.

"Very well." The clerk was obviously glad to hear that his smelly, unkempt guest had decided to leave his fine hostelry. "That will be fifteen dollars." Slocum took the rumpled five he had left from his gambling winnings and added one of Mrs. Durant's crisp bills to it. The clerk took the money as if it slithered across the desk in the mouth of a rattlesnake. "Thank you," he said with no conviction.

Slocum retrieved his paltry belongings, checked his Colt again, and then hurried off for the Proctor Point landing. He got there in time to see Petey and his friend come chugging up in a small steam-powered barge. Fresh hatchet marks on the hull showed where they had cast off in a hurry, cutting the ropes rather than untying them from the dock. Slocum wondered how long it would be before the owner came after it with a shotgun and the law.

He didn't much care as long as they got to the middle of the river in time to get aboard the *Pride of Orleans*.

"Where's the other two?" Petey called out.

"Don't worry. They'll be here," Slocum said. He began to wonder what he would do if Claudette Durant and her daughter didn't show. He didn't have enough money for the entire trip up the Mississippi, but the twenty he had left might be enough to get him started on the way.

Slocum heard the clatter of carriage wheels. Mrs. Durant drove with breakneck speed down the dusty road along the shore. She whipped the horse until its eyes showed white all around and foam lathered its sides.

"Sad way to treat an animal," observed the river man Slocum had never heard named. "Wouldn't do that if I owned the horse."

"It's yours when you get back," promised Slocum.

"Damn. Stolen, eh?" The man spat. "Get on board. I just heard the steamboat's whistle. We got to get a start on it or we'll never be able to overtake 'er."

Slocum went to the edge of the rotting dock to fetch Mrs. Durant. She reined in sharply and jumped from the carriage.

"Get us onto the river!" she cried. "We have no time to fritter away!" Her French accent came through strongly now. Slocum wondered what had got her so het up.

Mrs. Durant pushed past and hurried along the dock, not waiting for Slocum. He turned and heard a soft voice ask, "Are you going to help me down? Mama said she had hired a true gentleman to escort us upriver."

Slocum had thought Claudette Durant was beautiful. Her daughter was gorgeous.

"Oh, yes," the young woman said. "She *is* my mother. Everyone mistakes her for my sister."

"Seems like you're one good reason to start early into a marriage," Slocum said.

"Mama was right. You *are* gallant, in an unpolished frontier way." She smiled and Slocum thought the sun had risen twice that day.

"Come along," called Mrs. Durant. "They'll be upon us in a flash."

Slocum helped the young woman down from the carriage and asked, "What's your mother talking about? She came riding up here like a band of Sioux warriors was on your trail."

"It rather seems we were followed. Papa might have discovered our plans. However it happened, we have a dozen men chasing after us."

The words had hardly left her perfectly shaped mouth when Slocum heard the pounding of horses' hooves. He rushed down the dock and handed the young Miss Durant across to Petey. One cold look from Slocum made the man keep his hands to himself as he helped her into the steam barge.

A bullet whined past Slocum's ear. He ducked instinctively, spun and whipped out his Colt. The hammer came back and fell in a smooth motion. The gun bucked and brought down the lead rider. Slocum didn't figure he had done any real harm to the man—leastways, the man screamed curses more like he was angry rather than hurt.

"Sir, hurry!" Slocum heard the steam barge pull away from the dock. He fired twice more to keep the other approaching riders at bay, then turned and ran as hard as he could. He hit the end of the dock and sailed through the air.

Only Petey's strong grip kept him from taking another bath in the muddy river.

"Glad you made it," said Petey. "You ain't paid us yet."

The way both river men looked at the women told Slocum what pay they'd have extracted if he hadn't been able to reach the barge.

"There'll be something extra for this trip," he told them. From the shore came a volley of bullets that kicked up water spouts around the barge. "An extra ten dollars," he added, to make sure that they didn't misunderstand.

The *Pride of Orleans* sounded her whistle at the bend in the river. Slocum settled down to let the two river men position the barge for the mid-river transfer. His eyes locked with the cornflower-blue ones of Claudette

Durant's daughter. The young woman smiled in such a way that Slocum knew she was appreciative of all he had done.

Unless he missed his guess, the appreciation would extend to something more than money. Slocum decided the trip upriver might prove to be an interesting one.

7

"Faster!" John Slocum leaned forward as if this would help the steam-powered barge go faster. The *Pride of Orleans* edged away from them, heading for the middle of the river.

"Don't you go worryin' yourself none," came Petey's calm reassurance. "We'll get alongside her in a minute." He spat. "Might be two minutes."

"Might be never," grumbled his crony. "This tub ain't holdin' pressure too good. Boiler's leaking and it might blow us all to hell and back any second."

Slocum said nothing. If these two couldn't keep the barge running, he certainly stood no chance at it. He looked back at the shore and saw that Mrs. Durant's followers had not given up. They pushed out into the sluggish current in rowboats. It would take considerable effort for them to overcome the Mississippi's slow but powerful current, but they looked determined.

"They are very loyal to Papa," the younger woman said. "I do not like to think what they might do if they catch us." She shivered delicately and touched her lips with a lace handkerchief.

"They wouldn't do anything," answered Slocum. "Your safety is what they're more interested in."

"Hardly. Mama and I are...possessions. Papa is very acquisitive. He never loses anything he owns. We have no way of knowing what their orders are."

SLOCUM AND THE RED RIVER RENEGADES 65

He had nothing to say to this. She must know her own father better than Slocum ever could.

"You there. Give us a hand and stoke some more wood into the boiler. We're gonna make it to the steamboat if this barge's seams pop." The two river men worked like ten to overtake the *Pride of Orleans*. Slocum helped.

"Oh, look Mama. The steamboat is slowing. We *can* overtake it!" The young woman squealed with joy at the prospect.

Slocum worried about their safety. The metal boiler had turned cherry-red and rivets began to expand. In a few minutes they would be popping. When the sides of the boiler gave way, the entire barge would explode in flames. Even worse, he saw that the men in the rowboat had not given up the chase. Two bent their backs to row into the river's current. Going over the side to escape an explosion would only return the women to their hands.

He helped stoke the wood. The safety valve on the boiler began to vent steam. Petey reached up and jammed a long piece of wood against it to keep it closed. He turned and gave Slocum a broken-toothed grin. "We need all the speed we can get."

Slocum saw that they did overtake the *Pride of Orleans* slowly. Inch by agonizingly sluggish inch they narrowed the distance. When the barge banged against the steamboat's low side, Petey yelled out, "Get on board. We can't keep up with a paddlewheeler all day long!"

Slocum abandoned his post at the boiler and helped Claudette Durant and her daughter onto the boat. Eager roustabouts grabbed at them and dragged them over the cargo deck's low railing. Slocum fumbled in his pocket and pulled out the three tens he had left. He thrust them into Petey's hand.

"Thank you, mister. Get on off or you're gonna be stayin' with us, whether you like it or not."

Slocum saw that the man was right. He tipped his hat to them, then turned and jumped for all he was worth. His fingers curled around the rope at the edge of the deck. He slammed hard against the side of the *Pride of Orleans*, his feet in the water. The sternwheeler's draft was less than six feet, and the deck was hardly four above the waterline.

"Help me, dammit!" he called.

Slocum stared up into the muddy eyes of the barrel-chested roustabout he had seen blocking Mrs. Durant's way at the dock.

"Swim for it," the brawny man said. His heavy boot came down on Slocum's fingers.

Slocum swung to one side, getting his hand free to avoid the bone-crushing boot. He kicked hard and got one leg onto the deck. The roustabout kicked at him. Hard. Slocum gasped as the boot crashed into his side. Stars exploded in his hand from the pain. But he hung on. He dared not drop back into the river. Not only had Petey and his friend fallen back, the men in the rowboat still worked like fiends to catch up.

If the river didn't kill him, they would.

Slocum blocked the second kick by rolling onto his side. He grabbed the man's ankle and held on. He couldn't get to his feet, but the roustabout couldn't kick him, either.

Powerful hands reached down and grabbed Slocum's collar and pulled him erect. He looked up in time to see a quart of knuckles and fist cocking back to smash his face. Slocum ducked as the roustabout let loose the blow. If it had landed, he would have had his nose mashed all over his face. The fist slipped past Slocum's head and gave him the break he needed.

He brought his knee up as hard as he could into the roustabout's groin. The man gasped with the pain. Slocum worked his fingers under the man's belt and heaved as he twisted to one side. The air filled with cursing, moaning, thrashing roustabout. A loud splash marked his entry into the Mississippi.

Slocum sat down heavily on the deck and fought to catch his breath. His side ached horribly, but he didn't think any ribs were broken. He looked up to see a half dozen other deck hands standing quietly, watching him. One held a baling hook. Another idly tossed a knife from one hand to the other. Slocum tried not to appear obvious about checking his Colt.

He worried that the brief brush with the river might have fouled the charges. With the Colt Navy he could have taken all these men. Without it, he was dead meat.

"Never seen anybody outfight Rawley before," declared the nearest roustabout. "Reckon it was about time somebody gave him his come-uppance."

The river man turned and walked away. The others dispersed, no one saying a word. Slocum heaved a sigh of relief and went to find the two women. As he walked the ache left his side, but he knew he'd have one hell of a bruise.

The only consolation was that he had got the women aboard the *Pride of Orleans* safely and had removed a potential problem. He had no idea if Rawley worked for Benjamin Durant. If he did, he'd have to swim for Fargo.

Slocum climbed the steps leading to the upper decks. He stopped just outside the grand salon. Mrs. Durant argued with the paddlewheeler's captain.

"Any way I can help, ma'am?" Slocum asked. He spoke to the woman, but his eyes locked on the captain. When the riverboat was underway, the pilots were in command. Their sharp eyes tolerated no distractions; they were the absolute rulers of the boat. One small mistake and the boat could be run aground or sunk from a sandbar or river snags. But the captain's word was law in port, when it came to repair work on the paddlewheelers, and in all matters pertaining to cargo and passengers.

"The captain does not feel inclined to allow Nicole and me to remain aboard his riverboat."

Slocum almost asked who Nicole was, then figured she meant her daughter. He had never heard the younger woman's name before this. He covered this lack of knowledge and moved a step closer to the captain.

"What is the problem? I'm sure there's nothing we can't work out."

"No rooms available," the captain muttered.

"I'm sure there must be at least one for the ladies," Slocum said. "There might even be a pair of them. Or three, one for each of us. Want me to check and see which are occupied?"

He started to push past the captain. The shocked expression on the captain's face told the story. There were plenty of staterooms available.

"We can find suitable accommodations, I'm sure. I'll ask the purser to get on it right away."

He spun and stalked off. Slocum watched him go, satisfied.

"You will have to pay for your own room, sir," Mrs. Durant said. "You have enough of an advance against your services."

"Afraid I need passage money *and* some spending money," he corrected. "I used the fifty dollars to get us out here. That steam barge didn't come cheap."

"It was a wreck!"

"No argument on that point, but those two river rats gave us the transportation exactly when we needed it. That cost money." Slocum didn't bother mentioning that Petey and his friend had stolen the boat.

"Very well. I admit that we have not got off on a good footing." Her attitude showed that she wished she could dispense with Slocum altogether.

"How long will those men in the rowboat keep after us?" he asked. "I don't like waking up to surprises."

"They . . . they work for my husband. They will follow, but the next riverboat does not leave for almost a day."

Slocum frowned. The woman had no idea about how busy a river port St. Louis had become. Sternwheelers left for points both up- and down-river continually. Yet he had to admit she sounded certain. There was still more to her trip to Fargo than she had revealed.

"I will see to your passage and a room." Claudette Durant sniffed haughtily. "It will not be a first-class stateroom, however. A lesser accommodation will suffice, in your case."

"As long as I don't have to sleep on deck with the roustabouts," Slocum said, amused at her insistence that he was some lower form of life.

"That might not be a bad suggestion." The woman wrinkled her nose. Slocum knew he didn't smell too good after his brief dip in the muddy river and the work with the boiler, nor had he been rose-fragrant before that. He wanted to point out that he had saved her from the men trailing her. Slocum kept quiet, though. Arguing with the strong-willed, arrogant Claudette Durant wasn't likely to produce results.

She motioned to a white-linen-clad attendant and told him to fetch Slocum's luggage. To his surprise, the steward came back with the meager hoard. Slocum reckoned Petey must have tossed it onto the deck rather than into the barge's boiler.

He followed the steward past huge rooms bearing such fine, proud names as "The Texas Room" and "The Illinois Room." He caught a brief glimpse into one, The Missouri Room, and saw Nicole daintily unpacking. She looked up as he passed. The corners of her mouth turned upward in a fleeting, teasing smile. Slocum hurried on after the steward until they came to a narrow, unmarked wooden doorway.

"In here, sir," the black steward said. "Anything you need, you just ask."

"I'm in need of cleaning. Can you take care of it?" Slocum rummaged through his clothing until he found the tattered, dirty coat and the brocade vest he had worn when gambling in St. Louis.

"Surely can, sir," the steward said. "Might take a while to beat out the dirt, but I'll see that you get it back 'fore the gambling starts up in the main ballroom tonight."

"Much obliged."

Slocum turned around in the small room. It didn't hold a candle to the hotel room he'd just vacated, but he had no complaints. He went to the far wall and pulled back a wooden screen. Slocum smiled. This was the life. On the upper deck, he peered out across the Mississippi in an unparalleled view. For several minutes, he just watched the churning river flow past, other, smaller boats dancing along on their way in both directions.

He pulled himself away and closed the window. He had work to do. Before he did anything else, he checked his Colt and found that his suspicions had been right. Water had made the charges useless. If he had tried to fire, he might have gotten a wet *pop!* and nothing more. He cleaned the pistol and slung it in the soft leather cross-draw holster. He felt better, even if he needed a bath.

Slocum left the small room and went into the ballroom. Mirrors gleamed from sunshine coming in through stained-glass skylights. The highly polished wood, the crystal chandeliers, the broad dance floor, and the dais for the band all bespoke true elegance. He could never miss St. Louis in the midst of such luxury.

Touching his empty pocket reminded Slocum that he needed another advance on the money promised for seeing Mrs. Durant and her daughter north to Fargo. In the corner of the immense ballroom stood four green-felt-covered poker tables. Aboard a boat such as the *Pride of Orleans*, there had to be at least one greenhorn who didn't know odds.

The paddlewheeler lurched, sending Slocum to his knees. He came to his feet in a flash. The engines had reversed. Such a tactic required at least ten minutes of hard work by the boat's engineers; piston rods had to be removed and reinstalled. The only reasons for performing such a difficult chore were fear of running aground on a sandbar—and any decent pilot avoided the hidden 'bars in midday—or stopping for passengers.

Slocum had the gut feeling that the *Pride of Orleans* had slowed to take on the men who had chased them from Proctor's Point.

"What is it?" asked Nicole as she came out of her stateroom. "Why are we slowing?"

"Get back in your room and lock the door. I'll tell you when it's safe to come out."

"Oh!" The beautiful young woman ducked back into her room. The mahogany door slammed and a heavy brass bolt rammed home inside.

"Mr. Slocum," came Mrs. Durant's voice. "I looked out my stateroom and saw them. The men my husband sent are boarding the boat!"

"I'll take care of it." Slocum cursed to himself. He had grown complacent. Simply because they had beaten the men to the steamboat didn't mean pursuit would stop. And it hadn't.

He rushed out onto the upper level and peered over to the cargo deck. Three men argued with the cargo officer. One blew on his hands. Slocum guessed he might have developed a burning set of blisters from rowing so long to overtake the *Pride of Orleans*. That made him just a mite slower to fight, Slocum hoped.

The other two didn't look in better condition, but Slocum was hardly up to taking on all three.

He touched the Colt in its holster, then decided not to gun down the men. The captain had not willingly let him aboard. Any such massacre would result in Slocum's neck getting stretched by a rope tossed over a wooden cross member.

As that thought flashed through his head, an idea formed. Slocum rushed along the walkway until he came to a spot where he could drop onto the lower deck, using a pile of crates to get down. He went to a loading crane and swung it around. A heavy metal hook swung to and fro. He lowered the hook until it came to eye level.

Slocum rushed to where the three still argued with the deck officer. He acted as if he had made a mistake, stopped, and turned tail. The three men let out a whoop of joy and came after him. They were hounds hot on the rabbit's scent.

Or so they thought.

Slocum got back to the crane and whirled the metal hook around. The sharp point caught the lead man in the belly. He dropped as if Slocum had cut his legs out from under him with a cavalry saber. The second man dodged the swinging hook but slammed into a crate. The third vaulted the other two and rushed Slocum.

"Aiee!" The man's scream turned to a gurgle as Slocum sidestepped and stuck out a leg, sending him into the river. Slocum ducked the second man's swing, got a hand on the crane, and brought it around. The heavy hook struck the man in the back of the hand. Slocum grunted as he dragged him to the stern and heaved him after his friend.

"Freeze," came the cold command from the first man. He had drawn his pistol and had it leveled at Slocum's head. The bore looked large enough to sail the *Pride of Orleans* into.

"No need to get riled," Slocum said. "You were the ones doing the chasing. We just want to get on our way—peaceful-like."

"That's not what Mr. Durant wants." The hammer came back. Slocum knew he stared point-blank at death.

8

Slocum judged distances and knew he could never draw and fire in time to save himself. The man stuck his arm out straight with the pistol sighted in on Slocum's head. When the pistol fired, Slocum flinched. It took an instant for him to realize that the slug had gone wide. His hand flashed to the ebony handle of his Colt. He drew and fired in one swift, accurate motion.

The man tumbled forward, dead.

Slocum wasted no time. He went to the man and heaved him over the edge of the deck and into the water. He watched dispassionately as the churning from the paddlewheel bobbed the corpse around like a cork in the water. A heavy *thunk!* sounded as the body got caught up in the slowly turning wheel. A moment of bloody froth decorated the river, and then it returned to its normal mud color.

"I . . . I've never seen a man killed before," came Nicole Durant's shaky voice. In one hand she held a short length of wood.

Slocum saw then that she had saved him. She had swung the board like she'd been chopping wood. The blow had knocked the gunman's arm down, sending the deadly slug into the decking.

At this point Slocum had acted.

He went to the young woman and put his arms around her to quiet the sobs wracking her body. She dropped the stick and clung to him, her face buried in his shoulder.

"Did you have to k-kill him?" she sobbed out.

Slocum didn't answer. He had been kicked and beaten too much today to be able to take on three men and win without subterfuge or gunning them down. He worried about the shot bringing the deck officer or even the captain to investigate.

"Come on. Let's get back to your stateroom," he said. Nicole looked up, her bright blue eyes rimmed with tears. A tension between them mounted. Slocum bent and lightly kissed her on the lips. She flinched at first, then stopped and returned the kiss with a fervor he would never have thought possible from a proper young lady whose mother chilled souls with her very presence.

He pushed her ahead of him when he heard men stirring in the forest of bales and crates. A gruff voice rang out, "Heard a shot, I tell you, Cap'n. You wanted to know if those men what came on board caused a ruckus. I think they's responsible."

Slocum and Nicole skirted the edge of the deck, easing past the crates and getting themselves drenched in the spray from the paddlewheel. She vented a soft sigh that seemed to say that this wasn't her day. Slocum kept the young woman moving. He didn't want to do a lot of explaining to the captain about how the newly arrived passengers had got into a gunfight on the stern of his riverboat.

They trudged up the steps from the cargo deck to the second level. Slocum glanced inside the ballroom and saw a few men sitting at a poker table gambling for match sticks.

"Go straight to your room. Don't worry about them seeing you. I'll create a small diversion."

"Mr. Slocum," she said, her fingers tightening on his shirt and pulling him closer. "Don't leave me alone. I truly have never seen a man die before. And...and I helped. I didn't actually shoot him, but I *helped!*"

"Don't go getting hysterical," Slocum ordered sternly. "You'll be fine. Just do as I say."

"My door won't be locked—for you."

The expression on her face told Slocum what she meant. He felt a stirring in his loins that he couldn't deny. Joining Nicole Durant could mean only trouble. He knew better than to mix business and pleasure. Slocum also had to admit he had seldom seen a woman half as lovely as the blonde.

"Go on," he said. He had to decide such matters without her disturbing presence. He watched her slip into the ballroom and move slowly along the wall, hidden by shadows.

When she had reached the spot where she had to reveal herself to those in the room, Slocum burst in and cried, "Heard tell there's a big-stakes poker game in here. You the gents doing the playing?" He left damp footprints on the wood parquet floor and knew he looked like something the cat had dragged in. That guaranteed everyone stared at him and not at Nicole.

From the corner of his eye, Slocum saw the young woman rush for the door of the Missouri Room. She fumbled at the door for a moment, then ducked inside. Slocum heaved a sigh of relief. The gentlemen around the card table had not seen her.

"Sir," one said with some disapproval, "this is a small-stakes game." The man looked at his fellow players. They nodded in agreement. Slocum kept from smiling. What they meant was, they didn't socialize with riffraff like him.

"Sorry to have troubled you." Slocum nodded in their direction and set off for his room. He needed that bath and a change of clothing. With any luck, the steward had cleaned his coat and vest and done his best at repairing the rents in his fancy trousers.

SLOCUM AND THE RED RIVER RENEGADES 77

Slocum dropped onto his small bed and lay on his back, staring at the ceiling. Intricate patterns had been cut into the wood. Mythological characters chased one another and sported in forest settings. But Slocum saw nothing of this. His thoughts turned to Nicole Durant. She had saved his life by her quick thinking. After he had seen her reach the safety of her cabin, he had considered going over and knocking.

He knew the penny-ante gamblers would be watching him, though. To be seen entering a young lady's sleeping quarters would be reason enough for the captain to throw him overboard. Decorum was strictly observed aboard all Mississippi riverboats.

Even more of a concern, Slocum wasn't sure he ought to become involved with Nicole. Her mother appeared to have a mind of her own. From what he had seen, Claudette Durant also had a temper that knew no bounds. He had seen her bright blue eyes flashing with anger when she mentioned her husband. To oppose him as she was doing took uncommon courage.

Slocum doubted Mrs. Durant would draw the line when it came to protecting her daughter's honor from someone she considered a hired hand.

A rap at the door made him sit up. "Who is it?" His hand rested on the butt of his Colt. He wasn't going to go easily, if the captain had sent men to throw him overboard.

"Steward, sir. You wantin' some bath water? You looked to be in a mighty big need for it."

Slocum opened the door. The steward stood there grinning. "Seen what you done to those three men who came aboard," the steward said. "Reckon anyone who can do that to them needs a relaxing hot bath."

"You knew them?" Slocum was startled by this. He had thought the three to be common ruffians.

"Most everyone on the *Pride of Orleans* does," the steward said. Before Slocum could pursue this, the steward said in a loud voice, "Yes, sir. Right away. I'll go fetch that bath water for you." He turned and hurried off.

The captain and an officer stopped in front of Slocum's door. The captain eyed him critically. "Your trip satisfactory so far, Mr. Slocum?"

"Reckon it is, Captain, he answered. "What caused the lurch a while back?"

"Nothing. Nothing at all." The captain stalked off, chin held high to enhance his short stature. Slocum watched the officers go, wondering at the man's attitude. Whatever had put the burr under the man's saddle didn't seem to affect Slocum any. He went back into his small room and stretched. He had to see Mrs. Durant and get a few more dollars. The emptiness in his pockets bothered him.

The steward rapped smartly on the door and brought in a large tub of steaming water. "Anything else you need, sir?" The steward waited patiently.

"A big towel. Already got the soap." Slocum picked up a bar of soap beside the small washbasin in the room. The steward left. Slocum stripped off his grimy trail clothes and tossed them aside. After he had finished his own bath, he could wash them out.

He stretched again and then settled into the high-backed tub of hot water. The aches and pains began to vanish. He relaxed and started soaping himself into a lather. When a knock came at the door, he called out, "Bring the towel in and drape it over the back of the tub." He continued to work on the caked dirt.

The towel dropped over his shoulder. He turned to thank the steward. His eyebrows shot up in surprise. The steward was nowhere to be seen. Nicole Durant stood watching him. Her ruby lips parted and showed perfect white teeth as she smiled.

"Like what you see?" he asked. Slocum made no attempt to cover his nakedness. She could have shown her good manners and looked away. Instead, Nicole stared openly at him.

"You didn't come by my stateroom. You broke your promise."

"I was going to see how you were after I cleaned up. I smelled like a boar hog in a mud wallow."

"I wouldn't have minded," she said, dropping to her knees beside the tub. She took the soap from his hands. "Let me."

He didn't protest. When her slender fingers began stroking through his wet-lank black hair and across his cheek and neck, he felt himself begin to respond. Nicole's hands were quickly covered with soap—and she kept working her way down his body. He gasped when her fingers brushed lightly over his rigid organ. His manhood rose up just out of the bath water.

Gripping it firmly, she began stroking. Slocum gasped and leaned back in the tub. The young woman's agile fingers found all the right places to touch, to stroke, to excite.

"You like it, don't you?" she asked softly.

"Damned straight," he said.

"Yes, it is. And hard. And big. And ever so tasty looking."

He gasped when she bent over, her ash blonde hair falling into the bath. Her lips parted and found the sensitive tip. Nicole kissed him tenderly, then used her teeth on the sides of his shaft as her head sank down. He tried to control himself.

The feel of her lips moving along his lust-hardened length caused a quickening of his breath. Heart threatening to explode, he tried to tell her how much he liked what she did to him. The words jumbled in his throat.

His hips rose out of the bath in a vain attempt to sink even more deeply into her mouth.

"Naughty, naughty," she said. Lightly batting his manhood sent shivers of desire lancing into his loins.

Nicole did not resist when he reached out and pulled her closer. Their lips met in a long, deep kiss. The next thing he knew, she had hiked her skirt and straddled the tub.

"There," she said. "Do to me what I did to you."

He saw as she lifted her skirts ever higher that she did not wear any undergarments. With his soap-slippery hand he reached out and stroked over a mound covered with crinkly blonde fleece. Nicole moaned softly and thrust her flaring, womanly hips forward. He rotated the palm of his hand in slow, firm circles on her most intimate flesh. She sobbed and moaned constantly now. The slipperiness from the soap vanished and was replaced by her inner oils.

"I want more," she told him. She reached down into the water and found his still-throbbing length. "I want *this!*"

She lowered herself into the tub. Slocum didn't think she could do it, but she expertly fitted them together. Her legs went up over his shoulders so that her heels rested on the high back of the tub.

But it was lower that brought the tides of warmth to his loins. She completely surrounded him. When her inner muscles began twitching and squeezing, Slocum almost lost his mind.

"You like that?" she teased. "I can do more. Much more!" And she did. Nicole twisted from side to side, causing the water to slosh onto the cabin floor. Neither noticed or cared. Their passions mounted with every tiny movement she made.

He reached out and grasped her breasts through the thick fabric of her blouse. Beneath his fingers he felt the throbbing of her nipples as they turned to firm buttons. Slocum pressed down hard. This sparked even more movement.

She turned from side to side, then began lifting and falling about an inch. When she stayed relaxed, he penetrated her fully. This new movement hoisted her off him by an inch. The distance didn't matter. The way she clutched at him with her moist, intimate flesh did.

He began shoving her up and down faster and faster, seeking the rhythm that would light both their fuses. Slocum tried to hold down the fiery tide rising within him.

"Now," Nicole gasped. "Do it now! I need you so much!" She bent over and kissed him with all the craving locked within her slender body. They rocked together, driving each other toward a peak of sexual yearning.

His muscles tensed, and he could no longer hold back. His seed erupted into her hungrily squeezing interior. She threw back her head and gasped as passion seized her totally. Her blonde hair floated like a banner on a breeze. Only when the last explosive feelings had died within her did she open her eyes.

Nicole stared at him, her azure eyes slightly glazed with lust. "You are even better than I thought."

"Didn't do much," Slocum allowed. "Couldn't. Not like this." He was still pinned under her, one sleek calf resting on either shoulder.

"Then let's remedy that," Nicole said. She lithely rose and stripped off her skirts. "I seem to have gotten . . . wet." She licked her lips. Slocum had thought it impossible to respond so quickly after such lovemaking.

He was wrong. By the time he had risen from the bath and Nicole had completely stripped off her skirts, he was ready again.

This time was slower, less frantic—and even better. He decided this nursemaid job had decided advantages he had not known when he took it back in St. Louis.

9

Slocum straightened his vest and leaned back in the comfortable chair, his mind wandering from the game of Spanish monte. The other players knew little of the game and bet wildly. He had long since lost interest and only tried to prolong the game, taking small amounts rather than a single big killing. He figured this would win him the most in the long run without any animosity from the losers.

His thoughts turned to the past week aboard the *Pride of Orleans*—and the nights spent with Nicole. The blonde had proven an agile, willing, even wanton lover. He wondered what her mother would say if she knew. He held back a shudder. He had a good idea on that count. Claudette Durant wasn't the kind ever to forgive and forget. He had seen that repeatedly in the way she spoke of her husband. He had asked several times about Benjamin Durant and the reasons for seeking a divorce. Nicole had turned as tight-lipped as her mother on this touchy subject.

Slocum tossed a chip into the pot and won when the others folded. He raked in the few dollars in winnings, saying, "Time for me to take my daily constitutional, gents. Excuse me." One or two grumbled, but he walked off with less than five dollars from any single player. All told, Slocum was ahead almost thirty dollars for this session. The past few days had fattened his poke by over three hundred dollars.

In spite of winning back some of what he had lost in St. Louis, Slocum felt no satisfaction. His brother's watch still rode in Matthews's pocket. Until he recovered this only memento of Robert, he could never rest easy.

He went out onto the walkway circling the upper deck of the *Pride of Orleans* and leaned against the railing. The paddlewheeler had made good time up the Mississippi and into the Minnesota River. Within the hour they would reach port and turn around. From there, Slocum had to see the ladies across a narrow strip of land on the railroad to the Red River port. A new steamboat would be in soon, he hoped, and from there it was a short trip to Fargo.

He hated to see the trip over. True, he would receive the balance of his payment for acting as bodyguard—almost two hundred dollars, since he had taken an advance to use as a gambling stake. But he would sorely miss Nicole's nightly visits. When he had accepted the job, he had idly wondered what Claudette Durant would be like in bed. Her daughter had long since pushed such speculation from his mind. He had his hands full with the fiery vixen.

He shook his head in wonder. Outwardly, Nicole was the perfect lady. Get her away from her mother and she became a sex-starved wanton.

"Mr. Slocum, we reach the dock in less than one hour. I have prepared Mrs. Durant's belongings for portage." The captain pulled himself up to his full height and still the top of his head reached only to Slocum's chin. "She has instructed me that your quarters are to be . . . charged."

"Charged? What do you mean? She said she was taking care of my expenses." Slocum felt a moment's irritation. "Never mind. I have enough to cover everything."

"No, sir, you don't understand. She has asked that

your bill be charged against the *Pride of Orleans'* owner."

"I've missed something," he said, his mind racing.

The captain's eyebrows arched. "You've been with Mrs. Durant and her daughter for the entire trip and you don't know?" The captain's surprise turned to laughter. "This is a rich one!"

"Explain the joke to me," Slocum said coldly. He didn't like being the butt of a prank.

"Mrs. Durant's husband is Benjamin Durant."

"So? I know that."

"Mr. Durant *owns* this boat. He *owns* the Mississippi Shipping Company. He owns damned near every other paddlewheeler on the upper river and many along the Red River. She's paying for her own passage, but she is charging yours against Mr. Durant's account."

Slocum's anger vanished. In spite of himself, he smiled at the irony. Claudette had a sense of humor he had not fully appreciated. The man responsible for getting her to Fargo was being housed and fed by her soon-to-be-ex-husband.

"Those three men who came aboard after we'd left St. Louis," Slocum said. "Did they work for Mr. Durant?"

"Of course." The captain cleared his throat. "Don't rightly know what became of them after they got on board. Haven't seen them since."

"No one on the *Pride of Orleans* much likes Benjamin Durant, do they?"

The captain's smile turned to a sneer. "He's an arrogant bastard who would stab his own grandmother in the back for a nickel, and there's not a man-jack on board who wouldn't like to do to him what you've been doing to his daughter."

"I may have misjudged you, sir," said Slocum. He thrust out his hand. "Our interests seem to lie together, not apart."

The captain shook his hand firmly. "Be careful when you reach the Red River. Durant controls a fair bit of shipping on the river. He owns the drydocks in Fargo and a considerable portion of the economy owes everything to him from other concerns, and I heard tell he's tending personally to business up there."

"Thanks for the warning," said Slocum. His mind already cast forward. Getting to Fargo might prove more difficult than he'd anticipated. A man of Benjamin Durant's wealth and power never lightly gave up anything—especially a lovely wife and a gorgeous daughter.

He had known Durant wasn't keen on the idea of his wife getting away, but if everyone up and down the river owed something to the riverboat magnate, Slocum's chore might have become damned near impossible to finish. He was glad that he hadn't known about this from the start. It might have affected his decision to see it through—and he would have missed some mighty fine nights with Nicole.

"Mr. Slocum. There you are. What plans have you made for getting us to Fargo?" Claudette Durant strode up. He had not seen much of her during the trip, but then he had not been looking too hard. He had been occupied with keeping her daughter happy.

"The captain just told me your husband owns this boat. Why didn't you tell me?"

"It is of no concern to you or your job," she said, almost primly. She lifted her nose as if she had again detected a strange and ugly odor. "Benjamin owns many things."

"Those men I threw off the boat were coming after us. They tried to kill me. They would have kidnapped you and Nicole."

"Nicole told me about that sordid incident." She sniffed again. "It is like my husband to send thugs after me. It is a pity that the telegraph was ever invented—

and that my husband conducts so much business using it. That is neither here nor there. You are being well paid to protect us. I commend you for doing your job well. Now, what are you doing about transportation to Fargo?"

"We've got to take a spur line across to the Red River. From there we pick up another steamboat and go north into Fargo. What's your husband likely to do? I reckon he's sent out more men to stop us."

"He . . . Never mind." She held back a flood of angry words with great difficulty. "Once I have obtained my divorce, what he does is of no consequence."

"Getting it might be a problem. Some around here think he's already up in Fargo on business."

"His whereabouts were seldom revealed to me. Benjamin always came and went as he pleased. I chose this particular time to get the divorce because he was not in St. Louis."

Slocum frowned. Someone had sent the three men after them, unless they had been permanently assigned to follow Mrs. Durant. If that was true, Benjamin Durant might be more of a problem than he'd thought possible.

"I assume his minions have telegraphed him, wherever he might be," she continued. "What his orders might be I cannot say."

"Get the steward to put your luggage on the cargo deck. I want us to be the first ones off after we dock," said Slocum. His gut feelings began to tell him danger lay ahead—and not too far, either.

He lounged about until the *Pride of Orleans* came into dock with a gentle bump. Hefting his gear, Slocum went down the gangplank and straight to a ticketing agent. Through the grill, he saw a man with a translucent green eyeshade and a bored expression identical to the ticketing agent in St. Louis.

"I need to get a train over to the Red River," he said.

The ticket clerk blinked at him and didn't seem inclined to answer.

The man finally said, "You want the train station. Down the docks a ways. If'n you hurry, you can get the next one. Due to leave in about twenty minutes."

Slocum found himself caught up in a whirlwind of activity. He rented a wagon from a teamster and loaded the women's luggage. He helped them in and raced down the muddy street, whipping the horse mercilessly. He hated to mistreat an animal like this, but time played out on him. Twenty minutes, the clerk had said.

The feeling of impending disaster mounted, even though Slocum reined in at the same time the Great Northern train screeched to a halt in the station.

"You ladies wait here while I see to tickets."

"This is a filthy little town," said Mrs. Durant. She touched at the blonde hair curling from under her prim hat. "There must be fewer than one hundred people here."

"It's little more than a storage area for the farmers bringing their grain down to the river," said Slocum. "No reason to live here when the farmland is cheap and fertile." He hopped down and looked back up into the wagon box. Nicole shot him a smile that set his pulse pounding. He wondered where she got the fire. Her mother was nothing but ice.

He rushed into the train station and found a clerk who might have been the brother to the agent down at the docks. The man chewed on a plug of tobacco, got the piece off, and began to suck contentedly. When he got the first gobbet spit expertly into a brass spittoon, he said to Slocum, "Reckon you're wanting passage across to the Red River port. Nobody else comes through here."

"How much?"

"Real expensive this time of year. Ten dollars."

"I need three tickets," Slocum said. He mentally

added this to his bill. Mrs. Durant couldn't expect him to pay for everything out of his wages, and there didn't seem to be any way of charging this to Benjamin Durant's account.

"Got to warn you. The reason it's so damned expensive right now is the Indians. Damn Sioux are raiding up and down the Red River. Even shot up the train a couple of times. See that?" The man pointed to a white eagle feather.

"From a Sioux war bonnet?"

"You got a good eye. The engineer brought it back for me as a souvenir. They attacked this very train not a week ago. Didn't amount to spit, though. Never has, really. But the boats on the river, now, that's a different story."

Slocum impatiently looked at the train. The engineer had made his rounds with an oil can, making certain the cams and rods were well lubricated. Steam hissed as pressure built. It would be only a few minutes before the train pulled out. He shoved the three ten-dollar greenbacks across to the agent.

"No need to get your dander up," the clerk said. "Train's not pulling out till I give the say-so." He fumbled through a drawer and came out with three frayed cardboard tickets. The printing had long since worn off. "Give these to the conductor. He'll see that you're given first-class accommodations."

Slocum took the tickets and left without another word. He could guess what first class looked like on a short run. The trip wouldn't take over two hours.

He snorted. Two hours. Just long enough for a band of Sioux renegades to ambush the train. He didn't bother telling the women. It would only create a stir.

"You look to be in a foul mood, John," Nicole said softly. "What's wrong?"

"I just want to get to Fargo. Got business to tend to there."

"So do we. Mama is quite anxious to be free of Papa."

"What about you? You never said how you feel about this."

The sudden change in Nicole's attitude told him she wanted to cut free of her father too. In that instant she looked the spitting image of her mother, down to the firm-set jaw and the icy-cold eyes.

"Board!" called the conductor. Slocum heaved the luggage into a baggage car and passed over the three tickets. The conductor slipped them into his vest pocket for reuse. Nothing was wasted on this spur of the Great Northern.

Aboard and seated on hard wooden benches, they endured the train's protests as it pulled out. Even after it had built up speed, it continued to squeak and complain about the effort. Cinders flitted past the window like dark fireflies, but Slocum looked past them and into the countryside. The depressingly flat terrain promised plenty of warning if a Sioux raiding party attacked. He felt as if he could look all the way to the Pacific Ocean if he stood up straight.

"What's bothering you?" Nicole asked quietly when she saw they wouldn't be disturbed. Her mother had wrapped her arms around herself and sat in a tight little world of thought.

"I just want to be done with this."

"And me?"

"Not that. You're the best thing about this trip."

"Really? Prove it." Her hand slipped to his lap and began to stroke over his crotch. His eyes darted to Mrs. Durant. She was too far gone in contemplation to notice. But he wasn't going to take the chance. He caught Nicole's wrist and pulled her hand away.

"Spoilsport," she said, pouting.

Slocum got up and paced the length of the passenger car. No one else had boarded, and they had it to themselves. When the conductor came by, Slocum asked, "Any sign of trouble?"

"You been talkin' to old Johann, ain't you?" The conductor sniffed. "He likes to make mountains out of molehills. That feather don't mean we're gonna be stopped."

"But there have been raids along the Red River?"

"There have been," the conductor allowed. "Don't concern yourself with that. I'm sure you'll be fine." The way he spoke, though, told Slocum what the man really felt.

Slocum almost had to agree. They were fools for venturing into country where Sioux renegades ravaged at will.

He heaved a deep sigh of relief when they came into the station at the end of the spur line. If anything, this town was even smaller than the other. And like the other, it didn't have a name posted anywhere he could see.

"Please get us a stateroom on the next boat, Mr. Slocum. I have no desire to stay in this godforsaken place one second longer than necessary."

"Might not be any need, Mrs. Durant," he said. A steamboat loaded cargo for the two-hundred-mile trip to Fargo. It took him less than ten minutes to book passage on the *City of Moorhead*. Another ten saw the ladies' luggage stored in a single stateroom. Slocum would have to remain on deck, since the other sleeping rooms aboard the steamboat were being renovated.

He glanced into one and saw extensive fire damage. Stopping a passing steward, he asked, "What happened? What started the fire?"

The steward brushed a hand nervously through a thick shock of blond hair. "I am not supposed to say." He looked and saw no one in authority. In a low, husky voice almost incomprehensible due to his thick Swedish accent, he said, "The Indians. Renegades from the

Sioux reservations. They did this on our last trip upriver to Fargo!"

"You were lucky not to be burned down to water level," Slocum said. The fire damage was extensive. The smell of charred wood lingered, even though the entire outer wall of the stateroom was open to the air.

The *City of Moorhead* shuddered, and the heavy paddlewheel began turning. Slocum checked to see that his two charges were safely in their room. From outside the stateroom door he heard Mrs. Durant bitterly complaining about the accommodations. He smiled and went on. Compared to what her daughter must think about being robbed of her privacy—and any chance of lovemaking with him—this was nothing.

Slocum leaned on the upper rail and stared out across the barren prairie. It was hard to believe this was incredibly fertile farmland. Wheat, flax, and oats grew wherever the seeds were dropped. All he saw was flatness extending to the horizon. This was the sort of land he always wanted behind him. He had been through the Dakota Badlands a few times. The Black Hills held an attraction he couldn't deny.

He sobered at the memory of those hills. He had encountered more than one marauding band of Sioux in them. If they had left their reservation, that meant something stirred them to go back on the warpath. Their fierceness in battle impressed him so much that he would avoid them, given the chance.

"Are the ladies well tended, sir?" came a soft voice.

The riverboat captain stood behind him. "Believe they are, Cap'n," Slocum answered. "They're complaining a mite about sharing quarters, but seeing's how the *City of Moorhead* is lucky to be afloat, they're well enough taken care of."

Slocum studied the captain's expression. His face hardened, and his eyes turned bleak. Here was a man who had seen danger and death recently.

"You've been told of our problems."

"When did they start?"

"Almost two months back," the captain said. "We do what we can, but they strike at random."

"Never heard of an Indian who'd raid a riverboat. What do they want? Just to burn it to the waterline?"

"Sometimes. Last time, when we were afire, they boarded and stole everything in the boat's vault. They couldn't get the cargo—it was nothing more than pig iron headed north to be made into plows."

"Who's their war chief?"

"Can't rightly say."

Slocum started to speak, then fell silent. This was strange. The Sioux elected a war chief and made certain their enemies knew his identity. They believed rightly that this struck fear into the hearts of any they fought.

"We're looking to make this a quick, safe trip. We usually arrive in less than fifteen hours."

The *City of Moorhead* shuddered as the power generated in the boilers released and powered the paddlewheel. Slocum guessed that the captain ran the boat on the red line to make the trip in as little time as possible.

"The Red River doesn't look to have as many snags and sandbars in it as the Mississippi. That must help."

"Never run the Big Muddy. The Red River's dangerous enough for me, but you're right about the snags. Sandbars, though, abound. Excuse me, sir. I must go see if the pilot requires anything of me." The captain left Slocum to stare at the slowly passing countryside. Small, rolling hills developed, but still not enough to satisfy his need for mountains. He missed the Wasatch, in spite of his poor luck trapping there. When he got his brother's watch back, he might head directly west and into Montana.

As he pondered his future, the sun sank slowly into the direction he wanted to ride. The oppressive heat did not diminish; in this respect the Dakotas were like Missouri. Only the steady progress of the riverboat gave any hint of a cooling breeze.

Slocum tired of his vigil and went inside to find something to eat. Only a few oil lamps had been lighted in the large ballroom extending the length of the boat. It turned the interior into a coffin filled with spooks. Slocum involuntarily touched his Colt, then relaxed.

He went to find a steward and dinner.

When he was halfway across the dance floor, the *City of Moorhead* lurched so hard it threw him flat on his face. He slid and came to rest against the far wall. Dazed, he sat up.

Ghosts flitted across his field of vision. He almost laughed. His imagination was getting the better of him. Then his eyes focused, and he saw that the dimly seen phantasms were real. From one oil lamp he caught the reflection of war paint off a brave's cheeks.

His hand flashed to his Colt Navy. He drew and fired in one smooth motion. The Indian yelped, but Slocum knew that it came from surprise, not pain.

He got to his feet and rushed forward. Firing as he went, he came to a sliding stop outside the Durants' stateroom. Sounds of a struggle came from within. He spun, kicked in the door, and fired. A Sioux jerked back. Slocum had scored a direct hit on this one.

"John!" cried Nicole. "Help me!"

He plunged into the room, firing twice more. When his Colt's hammer fell on an empty cylinder, he tucked the six-shooter away in its holster and whipped out the thick-bladed knife he carried. To his surprise, the Indians fled, not wanting to face him.

"Mrs. Durant, are you all right?" Claudette lay sprawled across the large bed, her dress torn and her face scratched.

"I . . . yes, I'm unharmed. But what of Nicole? What have they done with my daughter?"

Slocum saw that the Indians had fled through the connecting door into the next stateroom. Of Nicole Durant he saw no trace.

The renegades had kidnapped her.

10

Slocum cautiously went into the next stateroom. The charred smell almost gagged him. In the darkness, he strained to hear the slightest movement. The only noise came from outside. He moved more quickly, but still took care. Sioux were sly when it came to ambushes. Falling into a trap now might forever doom Nicole—and leave his scalp hanging from a brave's belt.

He went to the outer wall and stepped over partially repaired timbers. The neighing of horses echoed up from the river banks. Throwing all caution to the winds, he went to the railing and looked over. On the cargo deck, half a dozen braves carried the struggling woman between them. Slocum saw the light from a small fire burning on deck catch Nicole's pale hair and reflect shimmering spots of brightness.

He acted without thinking. He vaulted the low railing and landed heavily behind the Indians. One Indian spun, his rifle coming about in a silvery arc. Slocum ducked under the barrel and drove forward, trying to find a sheath for his knife in Sioux flesh.

An explosion sounded, as if in the far distance. Slocum's movements turned to molasses. He tried to bring up his right arm and gut the Indian. His arm refused to move. His legs tried to keep him moving forward. His feet might as well have been nailed to the deck. Worst of all, his eyes refused to focus. He remembered falling, seeing the wooden planks rushing toward him. Then came all-enshrouding blackness.

Pain filled his world. Slocum struggled to fight it off, to push back the red curtains of agony drawing around him. In the distance he heard voices. He tried to persuade them, to plead for solitude. They came closer.

"... he'll be all right. The bullet only grazed his skull. One lucky buck, I'd say."

Slocum got his eyelids open. The light, though dim, burned in his head and made his eyes feel as if they would explode.

"He's coming around." This voice he recognized. Claudette Durant.

"What?" he started. Memories rushed back to him. He knew what had happened up to the point when he had been shot. "Where's Nicole?"

"The savages took her," said the riverboat captain. "There was nothing we could do. You fought well, sir."

"They took her." Mrs. Durant's voice carried none of the icy self-assurance it normally did. She had become a worried, frightened mother unable to do anything for her child.

He tried to sit up. Strong hands held him down. "You shouldn't be moving about, sir," said the captain. "We'll get you to Fargo and a doctor. Till then, you stay still."

"How long ago did they kidnap her?" Slocum felt strange vibrations. "The boat. Why is it shaking like this?"

"We grounded on a shallow sandbar. Them Indians came aboard whilst we were trying to pull free. The river in these parts is shallow and that's just the waves you're feeling."

"Then we're under full steam again?"

"Aye, that we are." The pride in the captain's voice took away Slocum's anger. The *City of Moorhead* rushed toward Fargo and left Nicole in the Indian's hands.

"I've got to get off." His strength had returned now. He shoved the captain away. Dizziness hit him, then faded. He wasn't as strong as before the bullet had run along the side of his head, but the more he moved about, the better he'd be. He had to get on the Sioux trail and rescue Nicole. The longer he waited, the less likely he was even to find the marauding war party.

"We're under way. You can't—" The captain saw the determination in Slocum's face.

"Don't worry, Mrs. Durant. I'll get her back." He took the woman's hands and held them for a moment. They had turned to icicles.

"The law..." Her words carried no conviction.

"I'll get her back and we will rejoin you before a day's out. I promise."

Slocum went to his gear and got more ammunition for his Colt. He would need all he could carry. Other than this, he took nothing.

"You won't find her," the captain said quietly. "It's cruel building up Mrs. Durant's hopes this way. And you? You're going to die, sir."

"Why hasn't the law gone after these renegades?" Slocum loaded his Colt Navy as he talked. "From all accounts, they've been a menace for several months."

"This part of the country's not got much in the way of lawmen. Getting up a posse to hunt them down is hard, too. This is the peak growing season. Men have their crops to tend. Besides, most of the killing and thieving has been along the Red River."

Slocum wondered at this. Robbing paddlewheelers had to be more difficult than stealing a few chickens from a dirt farmer. Still, there was no accounting for what went through a brave's mind. If they had left the reservations, they were out to earn warriors' names for themselves.

"We'll catch up within a few hours," Slocum said. "The Red River curves back on itself in a series of oxbows. That'll slow you down. We can cut straight across the country and be back aboard before the sun goes down again."

"Good luck," the captain said. His slumped shoulders and the expression on his face told that he didn't figure Slocum would ever be seen again.

The captain stopped the *City of Moorhead* long enough to put Slocum ashore in a small rowboat. Once ashore, he watched the riverboat get steam up again and begin its journey northward toward Fargo. On foot, alone, against a band of Sioux warriors, Slocum had no idea how he was going to prevail. But he would. Nicole Durant couldn't be left in the heathens' hands.

He started walking at a brisk clip, cutting inland toward a spot where the war party might have ridden if they headed toward the gently rolling hills he saw in the distance. The morning sun had yet to drive away the mist, but it felt warm against his back. He cursed even this small comfort. Tracking with the sun in front of him was easier. The light would reflect off the trail; this way, his shadow might cover important clues.

Slocum couldn't believe that luck had come his way this easily. The trail was obvious in the dew-wet grass. Shod hooves had cut the grass and left markings a blind man could follow. He knelt and studied the tracks. The Sioux must have stolen their horses; they seldom rode shod animals.

The juices from the crushed grass dried on his fingers. The trail was new—within the past few hours new. He started off at a dog trot, then slowed to a walk and built back up to a run to cover as much distance as possible without tiring unduly. Within a half hour, Slocum had another stroke of good fortune.

Grazing contentedly on the rangeland's sweet grass was a chestnut filly. He walked up to the horse slowly, not wanting to spook her. She looked up curiously, decided he was no threat, and went back to her morning meal.

Slocum grabbed up the reins dangling down and moved closer. She had been carrying a saddle not long ago. He saw the marks on her back and sides. What had become of it, though, was a mystery.

Slocum patted her head, then went around and vaulted up. The filly protested, then settled down. He wheeled her around and started on the Indians' trail once more.

"I don't know where you came from, old girl, but you surely do beat walking. My feet are sore and I hadn't been on the trail an hour."

The horse tried unsuccessfully to balk but soon learned that he wasn't going to leave. She settled down and Slocum turned his newfound steed in the direction taken by the Indians. By the time the sun had risen directly overhead and burned down with fierce summer intensity, Slocum was ready to take a break—and so were the Sioux.

He smiled crookedly when he saw signs that they had pitched a camp just over a low rise. A thin curl of white smoke rose in the still, humid heat. He dismounted and followed their trail on foot. A single white eagle feather caught his eye. He knelt and picked it up. Glue still clung to it.

After tying the filly to a low clump of sage, Slocum crept up the rise and lay flat when he reached the top. He heard voices coming from the renegades' campsite. Wriggling forward, he peered down into the camp, expecting to see sentries posted.

The entire raiding party hunkered down around the fire. The smell of brewing coffee made his nose wrinkle and his mouth water. But more curious than not finding sentries or the choice of brew was the way the camp had been laid out.

Slocum had seen more than one Sioux encampment.

This might have been mistaken for a white man's careless setup.

He inched closer. When one war-paint-and-feathers-bedecked brave stood, Slocum almost cried out in surprise. The paint was right. The eagle feathers were genuine. The Sioux brave was bogus. White skin instead of copper shone in the midday sun.

". . . came away with shit this time. He's gonna chew our asses good for it," came angry words. The leader gestured toward their tethered horses. "*That's* the only good thing about this."

In the middle of the horses on the ground sat Nicole, blindfolded and hands bound behind her back. She cowered each time a horse nuzzled her. Slocum wondered what these men had done to her.

"He's gonna be burned that we didn't get his wife, too."

Not only weren't these men Sioux renegades, they worked for Benjamin Durant—or at least it sounded that way.

"It's a sweet deal we got going," said the leader. He began rubbing off the war paint. They had little water in camp; he wiped the greasy paint onto his denims. Slocum wondered how he could have mistaken these men for Indians. Even in the dark and at the height of attack, he should have seen the difference.

But he hadn't. The captain of the *City of Moorhead*, the ticket clerks, the railroad conductor, everyone had been sure the raids were done by Sioux renegades. He had been duped into believing them before the attack. Who else should he have expected? Certainly not Benjamin Durant's henchmen. Mrs. Durant claimed not to know where her husband was.

He obviously knew more of her whereabouts than she did of his.

"Think we got a bonus coming for leaving her un-

SLOCUM AND THE RED RIVER RENEGADES 101

touched?" asked one man, lounging back on his bedroll and sipping at a tin cup of coffee.

"You'll get your balls cut off if you lay so much as a finger on her, Ned."

The leader presented Slocum only a profile, but the voice sounded familiar. He pushed this aside. He couldn't take the time to remember where he had seen the man before. Rescuing Nicole mattered most.

As much as he wanted to rush down with his Colt blazing, Slocum knew this would never work. Eight of the fake Indians stirred in the hot noonday sun. Better to wait and see if a better chance came along.

He sweated in the hot sun, the heat and gnats battering at his senses. But Slocum refused to slacken his vigilance. A chance might be lost if he let up for an instant.

His patience was rewarded. In less than an hour, their coffee finished, the phony renegade Sioux dropped off to sleep. Several snored loud enough to be heard up the rise. Slocum got to his feet and made his way down the hill. The horses in the remuda stirred at his approach. He moved more carefully. They went back to their nibbing at the rangeland grass.

"Nicole, stay quiet. We've got to get out of here pronto."

"John? Is that you?"

"Quiet." He dropped to his belly and wriggled forward. The nearest of the renegades stirred in restless sleep. Slocum got to the woman, pulled out his knife, and severed the ropes binding her hands. She almost collapsed with relief. He held her up and ripped the blindfold from her eyes. Squinting, she shaded her eyes with her hand.

"It *is* you! I hoped but it didn't seem possible."

"Can you ride?"

"To get away from *them*, I'd fly!"

Slocum smiled. He liked her spirit. "Riding will be

all we need to do. Let's pick a pair of strong horses and ride like hell out of here." He wished there was a way to get away quietly, but cutting two horses from the others without creating a stir wasn't possible. Their best chance for escape lay in surprise and speed.

"I rode on this one," Nicole said, patting a small black horse on the neck.

Slocum almost sneered. They hadn't even bothered to unsaddle the animal, much less brush it down. Stealing from the ersatz renegades would be a boon for the horses.

He found a strong gelding and swung into the saddle. The horse reared and protested loudly. This was all it took to awaken several in the camp.

"Horse thieves!" came the cry. "Some son of a bitch is stealin' our horses!"

Slocum drew his Colt and smoothly pulled back from the hammer. A round went singing through the camp. Although he hadn't aimed for it, the bullet struck the coffee pot and sent it flying through the the air, trailing a cloud of boiling liquid. This caused enough commotion that Slocum was able to get his horse under control and spook the others.

The rest of the remuda reared and pawed at the air. Slocum chanced another round. The loud report scattered the frightened horses to the four winds.

"Come on, Nicole!" he called out. "We've got to ride!"

"The girl. He's taking the goddamned girl!" This seemed to strike more fear into their hearts than losing their horses. Slocum heard the angry screams and curses as he bent low over the gelding's neck and urged the horse to a full gallop.

Bullets sang through the air inches away. He knew that any shooting at this range amounted to luck, not skill.

Even as the thought crossed his mind, he saw Nicole's horse falter, slow, and then stop entirely. He dragged back on his reins and shouted, "Come on! What's wrong?"

"I don't know. The horse just stopped." Even as she spoke, the horse's legs began to shake. With a loud gasp, the horse fell over on its side. The blonde managed to get her legs free and avoided being trapped under the dead weight.

Slocum rode back. A lucky shot had brought down the animal. He reached out and gave Nicole his hand. "Climb up. We've still got a lead on them."

"But, John, they'll be after us soon."

"Real soon," he amended. Several of the fake Sioux had retrieved their horses. "We've been lucky till now. Let's hope Lady Luck keeps smiling on us."

"Lucky? How can you say that?"

"We're still alive, aren't we?"

He put his heels into the gelding's flanks and started off at a brisk trot. To gallop with this much weight would tire the horse within a hundred yards. Brains, not speed, would get them free of the men chasing them.

"This isn't *too* bad, I suppose," Nicole said, her arms tightening around his waist. She snuggled closer and leaned her head against his shoulder. Slocum didn't protest. With her behind him, he didn't think the owlhoots would shoot. If they killed their boss's daughter, there would be hell to pay.

"We can circle and head back the way we came. I've got another horse waiting there."

"How did you find me so fast?" Nicole asked.

He started to say he'd been lucky. "The trail wasn't disguised. I picked up the spoor right away and it led directly to their camp. I should have known they weren't real Indians when I found the trail so quickly."

"They aren't Sioux? But . . ." Nicole's voice trailed off.

"You don't know them?"

"How should I know an Indian savage?"

"They're white men posing as Indians. If a posse is formed to stop the raids along the river, they'd never look for anyone who wasn't a Sioux. Even if the law found them on the prairie, they could always say they were a posse out to stop the renegades, too."

"I don't understand."

Slocum thought hard as they rode. He circled around to find where he had left the filly. He didn't expect Nicole to ride bareback, but they had to lessen the weight on this horse or it wouldn't be able to last another hour. It had been tired out when the fake Indians had camped for a noon meal.

Besides the obvious shield posing as Indians gave them, if the men worked for Benjamin Durant, it gave the shipping magnate a chance to ravage his opposition along the Red River. When they got to Fargo, he would have to check to see if Durant's shipping had been immune from attack. Slocum guessed that it had.

"There's the horse I left."

The filly stood impatiently, waiting for him to return. The sight of Slocum astride another horse seemed to insult the filly.

"I can't ride bareback," Nicole said.

"No need. I will. Can you control this one?"

"I'll have to." The blonde sat astraddle the horse and tugged tentatively at the reins.

"Damn. We didn't circle enough. Here they come!"

Coming over the rise from the camp boiled six of the fake Indians. They let out war whoops and waved rifles as if they were Sioux. But now that Slocum knew they weren't, the differences outweighed the similarities. They didn't ride anywhere near as well as an Indian, nor was their marksmanship the equal of a Sioux warrior's.

Slocum reached over to Nicole's horse and dragged a Winchester from the saddle sheath. He levered a shell

SLOCUM AND THE RED RIVER RENEGADES 105

into the chamber and fired. He missed the rider and hit the horse.

"Damn. I hate wasting good animals like that." He fired again, missing everyone. He settled down and squeezed off a good shot. One of the fake Indians yelped and fell from his saddle.

This sharpshooting turned aside their attack. They reined in and milled about, not wanting to continue.

"Ride!" ordered Slocum. "I'll hold them off. Get to the river and find the *City of Moorhead*. The captain's expecting us."

"I don't want to leave you, John."

"Then we'll die here together. Get going!"

He fired again, winging another. This broke their spirit. They turned tail and ran.

Slocum smiled and started after Nicole. With any luck, they'd have enough of a head start to reach the river and the steamboat and get to Fargo without any more trouble.

From the top of the hill he heard one man bellow, "Where is Matthews? We got to find him."

Slocum pulled back and glanced over his shoulder at the men milling about on the hillside. The man whose horse had been shot from under him got to his feet. The others circled around him, as if he was their leader.

Slocum fought the desire to rush back and find out if this was the man he sought. Was this Zebediah Matthews, and did he have Robert's watch?

He had come north to recover his property. This might be the chance he needed.

11

Indecision struck John Slocum. He saw Matthews on the hill, the silver conch belt glittering in the hot sun. He might be able to fight his way through and recover the watch. But in the distance he heard the pounding hooves of Nicole's horse. He had been hired to look after her—and that job went a damned slight further than simple duty. The woman's long blonde hair streamed out behind her like a garrison pennant. She bent over and worked to keep the gelding running toward the river.

He owed her a heap of protection. He owed her too much. Slocum wheeled his horse about and took off after her. The watch could wait. He knew that Matthews was in the area. That might be good enough.

If it wasn't, he could tell the law in Fargo about the fake Sioux renegades and get a posse after them. One way or the other, he would recover the stolen pocket watch.

"John, are they after us yet?" Nicole gasped.

"They will be soon enough," he called across to her. "They don't dare let either of us go."

"Why did they take me? Indians don't hold white women for ransom—and they never laid a hand on me."

"They aren't Indians," he said again. "You saw that. Those were white men posing as renegade Sioux."

He studied her profile as they raced along. Nicole

frowned as she tried to think through the problem. He didn't think she had recognized any of the men.

"Do you know Zebediah Matthews?" he asked.

"The name is familiar. Describe him for me."

Slocum did. "He works for your father," he went on.

"Oh, *him*. Yes, I know him." She wrinkled her nose and made an ugly face. "He's a tedious Englishman. Ever so odious, too. He is always making indecent proposals to me. Never anything blatant, of course, but the sly innuendo is sometimes worse. Yes, I know him." She turned and looked squarely at Slocum. "Is he one of the men back there?"

"He is. I heard someone call him by name."

"But if he works for Papa..."

"Your father hired them to kidnap you. Maybe he wanted to use you as leverage against your mother not to divorce him. Maybe it's something more. However you cut it, those were his henchmen."

"But they robbed the riverboat!"

"I reckon they're the ones who've been robbing most of the riverboats along the Red River."

"Papa always complained about competition. I didn't think he would go to such lengths to stifle it, though."

Slocum rode along in silence, wrapped in his own thoughts. Benjamin Durant must be a ruthless son of a bitch to order his own daughter kidnapped. Or perhaps he had ordered both his wife and daughter spirited away. He could keep them prisoners at some desolate place on the prairie until Claudette came to her senses and promised not to divorce him.

Slocum shook his head. There was no telling *what* the shipping magnate had up his sleeve. The man had shown himself to be a scoundrel. Where would he stop?

"John, my horse is slowing. Should I whip it faster?"

"No," he said. "Let's slow down. We won't get away if we kill the horses." He reined in. The horse neighed gratefully. Lather flecked its sides, and its nostrils flared with every powerful breath. Patting the horse's neck, he tried to estimate how much farther it was to the river.

"They didn't wait, did they?" Nicole asked.

"The *City of Moorhead*? No, the captain got it under steam, and they pushed on upriver. We'll have to cut due north and try to catch them at one of the big bends in the river."

"They travel too fast. How long has it been? I was kidnapped during the night. It's past noon now, isn't it?"

He glanced at the sun. It looked to be well past one in the afternoon. The riverboat had got underway just past dawn. Seven or eight hours of travel put it at least fifty miles farther up the Red River.

"Then we ride all the way into Fargo. It's not that far." He saw the expression cross her face. For her, it was too far. She was a gentlewoman, born and bred. She couldn't ride all day across a burning hot prairie.

The thought of the heat made Slocum's mouth turn even dryer than it already was. His belly rumbled from lack of food, and he wondered if they would find time to fetch food. Their pursuers might not let them have time to do anything but run like hell.

"That way. Now." He reined around and pointed to the north. He had no good idea where the Red River turned and went, but if they rode straight back they'd only be sitting ducks for Matthews. It was time for him to start concealing their trail.

"What are you doing?" Nicole stopped and watched him ripping a few low bushes up by the roots. He took a piece of rope from the lariat coiled and hanging from a saddle thong and tied it to the dried out bush.

"Here. Tie this to your saddle horn. Drag the bush behind, and it'll wipe out your horse's hoof prints."

"They won't be able to follow us!" Nicole's enthusiasm almost made him think it would work perfectly. He knew better, though. Matthews was nobody's fool. He might be a river man and a foreigner, but he had to know something about this country. Such a simple trick wouldn't throw him off the trail for long.

At least, Slocum didn't count on it to work for too long. But every minute he bought with his tricks got them that much closer to safety.

"We ride." The flatness of the terrain bothered him. The small rises gave scant concealment—and if Matthew got to the top of one, he could see for miles. Their best hope was the disarray in the fake renegades' camp. Given an hour or more, they might get away.

Slocum reckoned they had less than ten minutes before Matthews—or whoever headed the outfit—got control back and figured out what to do.

"If we got to the river and crossed it, wouldn't that hide our tracks even better?" asked the blonde. "I heard someone speaking of doing that once."

"You didn't take a good look at the river. It would take a ferry to get across. It looked deep to me."

"Actually, it must be rather shallow. Not more than ten feet deep. After all, didn't we run aground in the night? That provided the opportunity for the Indians to get aboard."

"You might have something there. Let's cut over in that direction." They angled toward the river again and within twenty minutes they came to its muddy banks.

Slocum's original concern proved all too real. The Red River flowed sluggishly toward the north, something he had to check for himself. He'd never seen another river this big heading in that direction, except for a few short oxbow turns. But the problem was in the width. To swim across with the horses was out of the question.

"Let's ride near the banks," he said. "We've got to keep moving."

"We can let the horses drink. They are tuckered out."

"The water's mighty muddy." Slocum shrugged. He had drunk worse-looking water himself. The horses gulped down the river water as if it was good. Pulling them away after a few minutes proved a task almost beyond him. His own thirst and hunger worked against him.

"You look a fright, John. And you've been injured!" Nicole dipped the hem of her skirt in the river and wrung it out before applying it to the graze he had got in the fight the night before. He winced as she worried the dried blood.

"We're going to have to ride on soon. We can't wait for them to catch up."

Nicole looked up, her blue eyes glowing. In a soft voice, she said, "You saved me. You didn't have to come for me."

"Yes, I did."

"Because Mama is paying you?"

"No."

She moved closer, her lush body pressing against his. They hesitated, as if both wanted to turn and flee. Then they kissed. It brought back all the fine nights he had spent with her on the way north. This more than anything else assured him he had done the right thing going after her.

Claudette Durant might be paying him, but he saw his duty as being more than fulfilling the terms of a contract.

Nicole broke off, her face flushed. "We really must ride on, shouldn't we?"

"Yes."

"But we'll have to stop for the night somewhere. The horses won't go on indefinitely without rest."

At this he laughed. He wished they were out on the prairie under different circumstances. With Matthews and the rest of Benjamin Durant's henchmen hot on their heels, they couldn't tarry. But he wanted to. The sight of Nicole's striking beauty made his heart pound.

"This is awful," she said, spitting out water from the river. "But I'm so thirsty. Is it safe to drink?"

"The fish don't seem to mind. The horses look fit enough after drinking, too." He knelt and scooped up a palmful of water and let it dampen his parched lips. Not for the first time he wished he had stolen a horse with gear, including a canteen filled with decent drinking water. But he hadn't. They would have to make do with what they had.

"Roll a pebble around in your mouth. Helps your thirst a mite," he said. Slocum took his own advice, rinsed a stone off in the muddy Red River and then popped it under his tongue.

"Really?" Nicole followed his lead skeptically. In a few minutes she smiled. "You're right!"

"Been living under worse conditions most of my life. You learn the little tricks for staying in one piece."

"I can imagine."

They rode in silence for almost fifteen minutes before Slocum reined in and turned to look behind. The river curled this way and that, but mostly it headed due north. Nowhere did he catch sight of a plume of smoke from the *City of Moorhead*'s stacks. The steamboat had left them far behind. They would have to go directly to Fargo.

In a way, this made it easier for Slocum. If they made a beeline for the boat, Matthews could follow directly. By taking a more roundabout course, they could lead him a merry chase.

Slocum unconsciously touched the butt of his Colt. He and the British river man had a score to settle.

"There, John. There's a road. Should we follow it?"

Slocum looked where the woman pointed. A deeply rutted dirt track cut through the low grass and went in for a direction that took them away from the river.

"Let's go," he said, deciding quickly. They needed to put as much distance between them and their pursuers as possible. When he found a better way of hiding their tracks, he would take it. Change tactics constantly, he thought. Keep Matthews off balance and unsure of their intentions. If it looked like they headed inland and away from the river, he might split his forces to cover both the trail and the Red River.

An hour of riding took them into gently rolling hills. The land was still far too flat for Slocum's liking. He could see for miles and miles—and Matthews would be able to, also. The dust cloud they kicked up on the road vanished when they cut across the grasslands, but they were too exposed. In spite of his worries, he saw no trace of pursuit.

By sundown he was too giddy to ride without swaying. His wound had sapped some energy from him, but the lack of food and water had done the worst damage.

"Time to stop. I don't think they're good enough to track us after dark," said Slocum. "I don't think Matthews is enough of a frontiersman to track us at all."

"He was in the British navy before Papa hired him. Rather, he was cashiered from their navy. He has never shown any skills other than those required along the docks." Nicole tipped her head back, nose in the air, in a way that reminded Slocum of her mother.

"We camp here," he said, dismounting. "There's a small pond which might provide something approaching fresh water. This time of day is good for hunting, too." The twilight-foraging creatures abounded. He had seen several rabbits who carelessly stopped to watch. The pond was a good spot to do some trapping. He was still leery of using his pistol; the report might carry for miles across the empty prairie.

"I'll get a fire going," she said.

"Here. Take them." He passed over a small tin of lucifers. Imagining Nicole trying to rub two sticks together Indian-style to start a fire was almost enough to make him laugh. Before he returned with a pair of rabbits, she had built a small, virtually smokeless fire.

He dressed out the rabbits and spitted them. After eating and swilling down the tepid pond water, he felt ready to whip his weight in wildcats.

For what Nicole had in mind, he needed all that energy—and more.

"Your fine clothing," she said in mock sympathy, running her fingers over the torn and dirty lapels of his jacket. "I'll tend to this immediately."

"And you're going to help me off with it, aren't you?" he asked, smiling. The woman quickly peeled the coat from his shoulders. He returned the favor, skinning her out of her blouse.

The next few minutes passed in a haze of building lust. Slocum never remembered tossing aside his gunbelt or getting his boots off. They lay side by side on a saddle blanket, the stars twinkling brightly above them. The warm fingers of a humid breeze lightly stroked over his body and kept the building sweat from distracting him.

His hand slid down the woman's naked front and found twin mounds of hot flesh. He squeezed. Nicole moaned as he fondled her breasts. The nipples turned to hard little points when he took them between his thumbs and forefingers and began rolling them in slow, erotic circles.

"More, John," she moaned softly. "I want more of you." They fumbled at what remained of each other's clothing and soon lay buck naked under the black velvet sky.

Slocum gasped when her nimble fingers slipped from his cheek to his chest and then moved much lower. She circled his hardening shaft and tugged gently. He got the message. He moved closer. Her white thighs parted wantonly for him.

"Now, John. I need you now. I've been riding all day thinking about this moment. I could hardly hold back."

"There's no need to now," he said. He silenced her with kisses. He reached down and ran his hands along the insides of her soft thighs, then worked his hands beneath her and lifted.

The blonde doubled up, her legs going high in the air and coming to rest on his shoulders. He wasted no time in moving forward. The tip of his manhood brushed across the moistness between her legs. For a moment, he held back, letting the tensions build between them. When he could no longer control himself, he slid forward, sinking into her hot, willing flesh.

A mighty shudder passed through Nicole. A lovely pink blush rose on her cheeks and shoulders. She closed her eyes and bit her lower lip. Reaching out, she touched his cheek, his lips, curled her fingers in his hair.

"Don't do this to me. Move, damn you. I want to feel you moving!"

He moved. His hips pulled back slightly. It felt as if she had clamped down firmly around his hidden length. He moved back in fully. In this position he began rolling his hips.

Faster and faster they strove together. Slocum trembled from the strain of controlling his passions. Nicole cried out her desires and clung to him fervently. As desire seized her totally, her muscles clamped on him until he thought he was trapped.

He pulled back, paused for an instant, and then slid back into her smoothly. He began the ages-old rhythm until his worries went away, and the world contracted only to the pleasures mounting in his body and Nicole's.

The heat built and the woman struggled under him. Her hands roved his chest, his sides, gripped his ass and pulled him powerfully inward. He began stroking with

SLOCUM AND THE RED RIVER RENEGADES 115

more power and speed. Nicole moaned in passion as new waves of desire seized her.

This proved too much for him. The hot tide of his seed rose and erupted into her.

Locked in passion, they rolled over and over. Only when he was spent did Slocum relax. His arms circled the woman. She had slid her legs off his shoulders, but had left them locked around his waist.

"You're not escaping that easily," she said with a lascivious smile on her lips. "I want more. Much more."

"Can't. Too tired. You really take it out of a man."

"We'll see."

Slocum hadn't thought it possible to respond again. He was wrong. By the time sunup came, he hadn't got much sleep—and he wasn't about to complain.

12

John Slocum shifted on the horse and tried to see through the haze covering the plains. He longed for the mountains, where a tad of elevation gave a decent view of the land. That didn't happen in the Dakotas. The flatness served to both hinder and help. If he couldn't see far, neither could Matthews and the others pursuing.

If they even pursued, he thought. There had been no sign of the fake renegades since he and Nicole had ridden from their camp. Slocum didn't understand this, even if the Sioux impersonators didn't cotton to riding across the country and exposing themselves to possible discovery. Matthews had been a sailor in the British navy. Slocum wondered if his fellows might not also be river men and sailors rather than plainsmen.

"Your father's hold on Fargo is pretty tight, isn't it?"

"What?" Nicole Durant looked at him, her expression unreadable. She had been lost in deep thought. He wondered what worried her so.

"If we go waltzing into Fargo, we're not likely to get far without it being reported to your father."

"I suppose not," she said. "I was thinking that we might be better off going across the Red River and into Minnesota. Moorhead isn't as beholding to Papa."

Slocum snorted. He had heard of similar situations. A town grew up on one side of the river and felt intense competition with a mirror image directly across from it. The name of the riverboat they had ridden from the portage gave a clue. The *City of Moorhead* meant something more than a name. It flaunted one city's independence of a rival.

"We can assume that the paddlewheeler has already made it to dock," Slocum said. "The spots along the river where we were most likely to have caught it were too dangerous for us."

"Mr. Matthews would have expected us to rejoin Mama." The blonde girl bit at her knuckle as she continued to think. Slocum wondered what schemes ran through her agile brain. He shook it off. He wasn't sure he wanted to know. He had to get Nicole back to her mother and see the divorce through. The remainder of his money would stake him again for another try at fur trapping in the winter.

He wiped sweat from his brow. His once-fine coat hung in dirty tatters and his britches had torn in several places. He looked less like a successful riverboat gambler than he did something dragged out of the river. A bath would be his first stop in Fargo—or Moorhead—and then he could tend to other business.

He went cold inside thinking about Matthews still having Robert's watch. What if the river bandit had sold it? Slocum decided he had to leave Matthews alive long enough to tell him what had happened to the watch if it wasn't in his possession when he caught up with him.

"There's a road we can take. I'm getting tired of the horse dancing around gopher holes." Slocum headed his horse due east along the red dirt road. In places water still stood and turned the dirt to a mud slicker than glass. He wasn't sure this amounted to a better ride than cutting across country, but it gave a sense of direction.

In less than an hour they stopped on the banks of the Red River.

"There's a ferry," Nicole said excitedly. "We can take it across to Minnesota and go up to Moorhead."

He nodded. It sounded like a fair plan to him. He

doubted Benjamin Durant's influence stopped at the river, but any breaks coming their way had to be taken. They rode the simple ferry across, the ferry man's eyes never leaving the lovely Nicole. Slocum considered letting the man try getting back across the river by swimming. A scuttled ferry would prevent Benjamin Durant from learning of his daughter's whereabouts for a few more hours. Slocum decided it didn't matter. If the ferry man didn't relay the information, someone else would.

Traveling with such a stunning beauty presented problems Slocum had never considered.

"Moorhead is less than an hour's ride to the north. We can follow the road," said Nicole. "I do hope Mama is all right. She tends to be flighty."

Slocum blinked. Of all the words to describe Mrs. Durant, flighty wasn't one of them. Seldom had he seen such a cold fish in human form.

"Your father wouldn't harm her. He just wants to keep her from getting a divorce."

The look Nicole shot him made him realize she was her mother's daughter. In spite of the hot summer day, he felt ten degrees chillier. Again he had found a spot where he knew nothing about the girl's life. Whatever she and her mother had against Benjamin Durant, it was immense and overpowering.

"I often wish I had no father," she said after they had ridden in silence for ten minutes. "He has done... things to me."

"Beat you?"

"No," Nicole said, laughing bitterly. "That he reserves for Mama. To me, he gives only tender, *loving* care." She looked at him with frightened, haunted eyes. The blue orbs that had danced with passion for him now held a forlorn and lost expression.

"You mean he—his own daughter?" Slocum had thought himself to be beyond shock. He had seen too much violence and blood since the war. Men cut in half by cannon fire, the atrocities Indians committed on white men, the awful crimes the white men did to Indians—there was no end to the cruelty and unthinking injustice. But what Nicole suggested outraged him.

"Sometimes he comes to me three or four times a week. Always just after midnight. Usually he has been drinking." She shuddered and pulled her arms tightly around her body, in spite of the increasing heat. "The times that he is sober are worse, though. I know he understands what he does to me then."

"Is this why your mother is divorcing him?"

Nicole shook her head. A soft, humid breeze from across the river caused a stray lock of ash-blonde hair to fall into her eyes. She never noticed. She rode with her eyes screwed shut so tight it made Slocum's heart ache.

"She might not even know. I've never told her." Tears rolled down the girl's cheeks and left dirty streaks. "I've never told anyone else."

"Why not?"

"How can I? It's so awful!"

To this he had no response.

"I tried to excuse it, at first. Then I . . . I just accepted it. It seemed wrong. As I got older, I knew it was wrong, and I was too frightened to speak of it. John, my papa is a dangerous, ruthless man."

The hatred boiling in Slocum's eyes convinced her there were other men in the world who matched her father's pitiless attitudes.

"Seems he has a lot to answer for," said Slocum. "And he will. I promise you that."

"Please, John. I just want to get away from him. There's been too much hurt already. Mama is returning home, and I am going with her."

"Home?"

"Back to France. She grew up in the south, along the Mediterranean. She speaks of it with such fondness. It must be beautiful."

A dust cloud ahead caught Slocum's attention. As they rode, he saw that it belonged to a small caravan of wagons laden with goods from town. The wagons creaked and groaned under their load as their drivers passed silently.

"Don't seem too talkative in these parts," observed Slocum.

"We don't look in the best of condition," she said, some of her cheerfulness returning. "They might think we are dangerous criminals come to pillage their fair town."

"Have you ever been here before?"

"No, but I've heard Papa speak of it so much I almost feel that I have. This is how Mama came to know of Fargo's reputation as a divorce-granting center. Papa all the time went on about how his men would marry soiled doves along the Missouri and Mississippi and then hurry here for a quick divorce."

They rode into the center of Moorhead, but Slocum indicated that they should go directly to the ferry. As he sat astride his horse, he saw the *City of Moorhead* docked across the river. From the activity aboard the paddlewheeler, he guessed that it had docked at least an hour earlier. Much of the cargo had been unloaded and some new crates were being wrestled aboard by the roustabouts.

"There's no sense hiding our heads in the sand over here when the action is there." He pointed toward Fargo. "Your mother's not likely to find us on this side and she might be getting a mite frantic about you."

"We can send a message to her. I . . . I don't want to go across."

"You that frightened of your papa?"

She could only nod.

"I reckon he is there. And I reckon the time's about right to meet him face to face. Men like him throw their weight around and think they can get by doing it forever."

"Please, John. This is not necessary."

Slocum had already signalled to another ferry man that they wanted passage across the Red River. He urged his horse forward onto the small barge and waited for Nicole to decide. With some reluctance, she joined him.

"It's better if Mama gets her divorce and then leaves town. There will be time to join her."

"Now," Slocum said firmly. Nicole didn't speak to him all the way across the turbulent river. On the other side, they led their horses up the bank and to a broad street with a crudely lettered sign proclaiming it to be Front Street. From the activity along the street, it had to be the major street going through the town.

"Where do we go from here?" asked Nicole. She looked frightened. Every passing wagon or man with a horse caused her to start. Slocum had never seen her appear so young or so vulnerable.

"A hotel. There's one down the street a ways."

A sign needing paint told Slocum this was the Sherman House. He checked the crossing street. Seventh.

"Doesn't look like the kind of place Mama would stay."

"Don't reckon so," said Slocum. "But that one does." He led his horse in the direction of a four-story-tall structure on the next street over.

"NP Avenue," read Nicole. "That must mean the Northern Pacific."

"Why so outraged at the idea? The railroad's been in this town for some time. The Headquarters House there doubles as depot for the rail line and a hotel."

Nicole started to ask how he knew, then saw the ornately lettered signs proclaiming all Slocum had said. She straightened her dress and failed to smooth out any of the wrinkles.

"That is the type of place Mama would go."

"Rates are two or three dollars a day. Downright expensive for someone not sent by the NP Railroad, I'd say." The money Slocum carried burned a hole in his pocket. Even as he tethered his horse outside the posh hotel he imagined the feel of hot, soapy water on his skin.

"Papa says the railroad is destroying his business."

"What difference does that make to you?"

"None, I suppose." She brightened. "Staying here helps the railroad and takes money from Papa. I like that notion!"

"After the divorce, you can get on a train and head back East," said Slocum. He wondered at the brief pang he felt at this. Did he want to go with Nicole? Did he want her to stay? They had enjoyed each other's company on the *Pride of Orleans* and out on the prairie, but did he want to continue?

He found himself wondering about that.

His attention snapped back to the hotel lobby when he heard Nicole cry out, "Mama!"

The girl rushed into the immense lobby and threw her arms around Claudette Durant. Slocum almost laughed at the look of disapproval the older woman gave her wayward daughter. Such filth could not be tolerated.

"Mr. Slocum saved me, Mama. They looked like renegade Indians but they were white men and John tracked them down and rescued me and we rode and missed the steamboat and came right on in to Fargo." Nicole stopped to suck in a much-needed breath.

"Mr. Slocum, you seem to have proven your worth in this matter." Nothing cracked the woman's stony exterior.

"Yes, ma'am."

"Then everything is proceeding well. The *City of Moorhead* arrived some three hours ago. I came immediately to this hotel and commenced my search for a lawyer."

Slocum marveled at her persistence in pursuit of marital freedom.

"I located a Jonathan Kinsbury, Esq., who took my case. For a large fee, he has guaranteed that the divorce will be final when court opens tomorrow morning."

Slocum blinked at this unseemly haste. He scratched his chin. "Reckon you're getting what you're paying for then, Mrs. Durant."

"Of course I am. Come along, Nicole. You must change out of those filthy rags and into something decent. I have reserved a table for dinner, and you cannot show up looking like this."

"Mrs. Durant, a moment."

"Yes, Mr. Slocum?"

"Seeing's how you have everything under control and you've got your daughter back, why not pay me the balance owed and let me be on my way?"

"A splendid idea."

"Mama, wait..."

Mrs. Durant paid no attention to her daughter's protests. She fumbled in her sequined clutch purse and withdrew a large roll of greenbacks. "I paid Mr. Kinsbury one thousand dollars for his services. I have received equal devotion from you, sir. Here is the balance of your payment, plus a five-hundred-dollar bonus."

"That's generous of you, ma'am." Slocum fingered the money, then looked Nicole square in the eye. "But you keep your bonus money. No amount can pay me for getting her back. It was my pleasure saving your daughter."

"Your rude exterior does not betray your gentlemanly qualities, sir. Thank you." Claudette Durant turned and took her daughter's elbow to escort her to a broad staircase. She froze when a deep-throated bellow filled the huge lobby.

"Where'n the bloody hell's my wife?" The front doors rattled and glass tinkled as it broke from the force of being thrown open.

Slocum didn't have to be told the portly man with the walrus mustache and gold-headed walking cane was Benjamin Durant.

13

"I just got into this flea-bitten, godforsaken town and find my wife sneaking behind my back. What'n the hell are you doing here?" Benjamin Durant stormed across the lobby, shoving people out of his way. One man started to protest. The gold-headed cane rose and fell in a short, vicious arc. The man crumpled to the floor, clutching his bleeding head.

"Go up to the room, Nicole," Mrs. Durant ordered. The girl took only a single step before her father caught her. His meaty hand grabbed her upper arm and spun her around.

"You stay here. I don't want any of you running off."

Slocum saw the stark fear on Nicole's face. She was terrified of her father. Slocum hadn't known if her story had carried any truth to it. She might have been lying to him to win sympathy. He had never figured out how the wealthy thought or acted. But the fear etched on her beautiful face told the story.

All she had said about her father was true—and she might not have told everything.

"You're not supposed to travel without my permission. When the clerk back in St. Loo telegraphed me that you'd booked passage on the *Pride* I damned near had him thrown into the river."

"We'll do anything we please." Mrs. Durant put up a brave front, but Slocum saw how incapable she was of withstanding her husband's anger.

125

He couldn't fault her for that. This was no ordinary man. He radiated power that didn't come from money. Added to the obvious wealth he controlled, Benjamin Durant was a formidable opponent.

Slocum had collected his money; he had fulfilled the letter of his contract with Claudette Durant by getting them safely to Fargo. He need only walk out the door and let the family fight continue.

He grabbed Durant's wrist and twisted sharply. The shipping magnate screeched, more in surprise than in pain. He released his grip on Nicole and swung around to face Slocum.

"Who'n the bloody hell are you?"

"I don't like seeing anyone mistreat a woman. You were hurting her."

"She's my damned daughter, and I'll do with her as I please!"

"That's what I've heard."

Durant's ruddy face clouded with anger, and his thick walrus mustache began to tremble. He shoved out his belly and bounced against Slocum's wiry, whipcord frame. Slocum didn't move an inch. Face to face, the two men stared at each other, each waiting for a sign of weakness.

Benjamin Durant found none in Slocum's cold green eyes.

"Men like you end up floating face down in the river."

"The ladies have an appointment. Let them keep it."

Slocum sensed rather than saw Durant bringing the gold-headed cane around. He turned slightly and caught the heavy stick on his thigh. The blow was aimed at his crotch; it sent lances of pain burning into his upper leg. He stumbled back. Durant swung a hamlike fist that connected squarely on the side of Slocum's head. He went tumbling to the floor.

"Reach for that six-shooter and I'll see you hanging."

"I don't need it," said Slocum. He rolled to the left, then quickly reversed in time to avoid a well-shined boot in the side. He came to his feet, ready to fight. Ducking under a wild swing of the cane, Slocum moved in. His fists pumped hard and fast into Durant's midsection. For all the appearance of fat, Durant's gut was hard. This didn't stop Slocum's attack. He got in four devastating punches before Durant gasped and backed off.

Slocum had the advantage. To quit meant defeat. He followed. One punch caught Durant on the ear. As the shipping magnate's head swung about, Slocum measured him and drove his right squarely into the center of his face. Crushing nose and splitting lip sent a shower of blood over both men.

"Here now, what's going on? We can't have fighting in the NP depot!"

A squad of Northern Pacific workers led by the stationmaster rushed forward. Slocum looked from them back to Durant. The man still swayed. A final roundhouse swing sent Durant to the floor, arms outstretched and unconscious.

"Nothing to get your dander up over," said Slocum, panting. He wiped his bloodied knuckles on his coat.

"We're gonna hafta call the sheriff," said the stationmaster when he saw who Slocum had knocked out. "Mr. Durant's right powerful man in these parts."

"He is my husband, and he is a brute," spoke up Claudette Durant.

"Don't reckon you'd find anyone around here who'd argue the point," said the stationmaster. "It might just be that he stumbled and fell and no one saw what happened."

Slocum nodded in the man's direction. Durant hadn't won any friends in Fargo, especially with the Northern Pacific Railroad workers. The rail and the steamboat lines were in direct competition. There was no telling what dirty tricks Durant had used against the NP.

"We can tend you in our room," said Nicole. The girl's blue eyes flashed when her mother started to object. Slocum smiled crookedly. A steel will ran through the Durant family. He had seen it more than once in Nicole. Standing up to her mother after such an unpleasant confrontation with her father proved her courage—if Slocum needed any further proof.

Slocum motioned her away and went to the clerk behind the long, polished mahogany counter. "A room for two nights," Slocum announced, loud enough for everyone to hear. He pulled out his roll of greenbacks and peeled off a ten. "And prepare a hot bath. I'll have need of new clothing, also."

"As you wish, sir. Will there be anything else?" The clerk passed over a room key with a large wooden fob attached.

"Send up some food. I've just tangled with the Sioux renegades." Slocum looked pointedly at Durant, who struggled to sit up. The man heard enough of what Slocum had said for his already florid face to turn even darker shades of red. Of those in the room, only Durant, his daughter, and Slocum knew who was behind the Red River renegades.

Slocum spun and walked off. As he went up the stairs, Claudette on one side and Nicole clinging to his arm on the other, his back itched. Did Durant pull a hide-out pistol and draw a bead on the back of his enemy? Slocum strained to hear any hint of such a move. The others in the room mumbled about his bravery—or stupidity—in facing down the shipping magnate the way he had. But he heard nothing to warn him.

At the landing, he turned and went up another flight. From the corner of his eye he saw that Durant had left the lobby.

"No one's ever stood up to Benjamin like that," said Mrs. Durant. "He will not tolerate it."

"He won't even have to like it," answered Slocum. "After tomorrow morning, you'll be free of him."

"I had not hired you to protect us after we arrived. I did not think there would be any difficulty once we were in Fargo."

"Consider this a bonus. I never liked bullies."

Nicole squeezed down hard on his arm and rested her head against his shoulder as they walked. Slocum couldn't tell if her mother approved—or even saw. Mrs. Durant walked with her eyes fixed straight ahead and her expression set as hard and cold as any marble statue. She stopped in front of a room and made a vague gesture in the direction of Nicole.

"Mama wants me," the girl said softly. "I'll be by your room when I get her settled."

"No, don't," Slocum said, sharper than he had wanted. She pulled back and stared at him, blue eyes wide. "I've got unfinished business."

"Not with me?" The coquettish look returned. She batted her eyelashes in a way that must have melted men's hearts in St. Louis high society. Slocum would have relented if he hadn't had unfinished business with Benjamin Durant.

Slocum sneered slightly. That wasn't the only business he had left undone, either. Zebediah Matthews still walked around free as a bird and sporting a stolen watch.

"Later, John." Nicole slipped away. He wasn't certain if she had meant that as a question or a statement.

He walked down the corridor, turned, and walked for what seemed a year until he came to his room. He went in and found quarters more than he had anticipated. A big bed dominated the center of the room. Beveled glass caught the rays of the sun and sent rainbows everywhere. His nose wrinkled as he sniffed. The room had been perfumed. The velvet drapes pulled back fully to reveal a set of French doors leading out onto a balcony overlooking NP Avenue.

Somewhere out in Fargo Durant plotted and schemed. It wouldn't take the corpulent man long to figure out the best way of getting his wife back and eliminating Slocum. Durant had the air of a man who got things done.

Slocum answered the soft knock on the door and admitted a bellman with a galvanized bathtub. In a few minutes, steaming water had been poured into it and a cake of soap had been brought.

"Clothing is being sent up, sir. I think we have found something that will fit." The bellman waited. Slocum peeled off a pair of tens and gave them to him. The man nodded and vanished.

Slocum placed his Colt Navy beside the tub, then stripped and sank into the water. It stung his hide but he didn't move. In a few minutes he began to feel almost human again. The aches and pains vanished and the grime washed away. By the time he had finished ablutions, another bellman arrived with the clothing. Slocum chased the man off, got dressed, and was pleasantly surprised at the quality and fit. The coat wasn't as elegant as the one he had worn on the riverboat, but it was serviceable. The britches rode up and cut him a mite on the crotch, but the important items suited him just fine.

He could reach his cross-draw holster and the Colt it carried in a hurry without the swallowtail coat getting in the way.

Adjusting the tilt of his hat, Slocum went out onto the balcony and peered into the street. Across from the Headquarters House loitered a half dozen river men. They idly carved on pieces of wood and matched coins to kill the time. Slocum guessed an equal number were posted out back—and all were Durant's men. If he poked his nose out of the hotel, they'd be more than willing to cut it off.

He moved back until he pressed along the wall and went the length of the hotel to the end of the balcony. Drainpipes ran from the roof and gutters to water barrels in the alley. Slocum swung out and dropped down the story to the ground and dusted himself off. No one noticed him as he slipped into the street and walked slowly away from the hotel.

Slocum had to force himself not to draw and fire the instant he saw Matthews going into a building on Washington Street, not three blocks from the Headquarters House. Slocum looked up and down the street, wondering what struck him as odd. It finally occurred to him. He didn't see any saloons.

He went to the doorway and looked into the building. It might have been a social club. Small parlors radiated from the central lobby and two narrow staircases on either side of the room spiralled up to the second floor and a mezzanine. Patrolling there Slocum spotted two men armed with shotguns.

Curious about the sort of place Matthews had entered, Slocum scouted the outside. No business sign told him what went on inside, though he could guess. It might be a whorehouse, but it was different from anything he had ever seen.

The rumble of wagon wheels made him duck into a doorway when he reached the alley behind the building. Two men jumped down from the wagon and began unloading unmarked cases that sloshed and gurgled.

Slocum saw no one else nearby. He moved from the safety of the doorway and went to the men. "What are you carrying today?" he asked.

"Same as always," one replied, not even looking up. "Ten cases of whiskey."

The second man emerged from the rear door and called out, "Who are you? What you wantin', mister?"

"Curiousity is getting the best of me," Slocum admitted. "Isn't this a saloon?"

"You just blow into town?"

"Just fell off the turnip wagon," conceded Slocum. The men laughed at this.

"They got laws in this God-fearing community. It's dry."

"So you're bootleggers?"

"Hardly. We live over in Moorhead. Wet there. We run a legitimate business. What they do with the liquor after we deliver it is *their* business."

"This is a private club?"

"Private, maybe, but not too picky about who they let in." The first man sniffed. "Too damn many of Durant's thugs here, if you ask me."

"That wouldn't be Ben Durant, now would it? I heard tell he runs Fargo. Owns most of it outright."

"If he don't, it ain't for lack of trying. After the NP went bust back in the Panic of '73, he tried to run 'em out of town. Ain't nobody gonna run the railroads out once they got a foothold."

"Especially not some river man," cut in the second man.

"You don't cotton to river men, do you?"

"Bloody thieves, the lot of 'em." The man spat. "The railroaders played fair with us. Bought land cheap from them, and they give us good rates on getting our grain to market. Not those waterlogged bastards." He spat again.

They saw that Slocum appreciated their opinions and didn't seem too riled. The second man went on. "Been here well nigh seven years. Reason Fargo's dry is old man Durant. He wants to supply all the liquor himself. Can't do it. He gave up a few years back when me and Jake started our business. That don't mean he lets up none on the teetotaler law, though."

"Keeping Fargo dry means more money for us," Jake

said. "Him, too. We got to pay a tariff, he calls it, on each place we supply. Not too much or we'd find ways around it, but enough that it galls me."

"We got rounds to make. You want to go on in, mister, why not do it now? Nobody's gonna ask how you got in. And the whiskey's good, even if the company ain't."

The men clambered aboard their wagon and left amid rattles and clanks and creaking wheels.

Slocum waited until they had rounded the corner before slipping into the back door. The storage room was piled high with crates of booze. Slocum guessed that Durant ran a supply business of his own to places in Fargo Jake and his partner knew nothing about.

He slowly opened the inner door and peered into a kitchen. The cook lay sprawled on the table, snoring loudly. A half-empty bottle of rotgut stood on the table near his hand. Slocum saw that the man had drunk himself into a stupor. Moving more quickly, he went through the kitchen and into the main parlor in search of Matthews.

The British sailor's voice carried throughout the building as he argued with another in a side room. Slocum glanced above. The patrolling guards were taking a break and were nowhere to be seen.

His ebony-handled Colt slid smoothly from the soft leather holster. He would get his brother's watch back or know the reason.

14

John Slocum paused when he heard what Matthews said inside the parlor room.

"I tell you, there's not enough bleedin' booty to make this worth our while," the British sailor said. "We got no choice."

"But Zeb, double-crossing Mr. Durant is dangerous. He got this whole town—the whole damn territory!—in his hip pocket."

"He may own this hunk of good-for-nothing dirt, but he don't own the *world*. We can take what we want and leave. Sail the seas. Get off the muddy rivers and out onto the briny where sailors belong."

"We ain't sailors, Zeb," spoke up a third man. "We belong on the river. Nothing's better'n to be sailin' along under moonlight and seein' the Mississippi all lit up right purty."

"You aren't men," snapped Matthews. "You're cowards. You got custard for guts. He's broke your spirit right good, I'd wager."

"We can't cross him."

"I can. I will. I'm gonna tell the marshal who's behind the Indian thievery along the river."

"Mr. Durant'll kill you for sure, if you do that, Matthews."

Slocum heard the tone change. The two men with Matthews didn't have his stomach for betraying their employer. From all he had learned of Benjamin Durant, stepping on an angry rattler might be safer.

That was neither here nor there for Slocum. He wanted his brother's watch back.

He spun and stood in the doorway, Colt leveled and cocked and ready to blow the head off anyone stirring. For the span of a heartbeat, no one in the room moved. Zebediah Matthews was the first to recover.

"What 'ave we got here? If it ain't Mrs. Durant's pet lapdog. You come sniffin' 'round the wrong place this time, bloke."

Slocum lifted his pistol and aimed directly between Matthews's eyes. "That watch chain dangling from your vest pocket. Tug on it real easy and get the watch out."

"You're robbin' me?" Matthews rocked back in his chair, confused. A grin spread over his face like scum floating on a pond. "You've got the sense of humor, now don't you, mate?"

"The watch. Take it out."

"You'd shoot me down if I didn't?" The grin vanished when Matthews saw that Slocum would. "What's so bloody important about this watch? I took it off a bloke back in St. Louis."

Even as the words left his lips, realization hit Matthews.

"You! You're the one I stole it from! You're the bloke who's been bird-dogging me every step, too."

"You look better in the fake Indian war paint than you ever would with a bullet hole between your eyes."

Slocum's finger tightened on the trigger, but the bullet didn't blow off Matthews's head. He ducked and swung about, the six-shooter pointing back into the lobby. The Colt bucked and sent leaden death into the gut of a man who was levelling a shotgun at his back.

This diversion sent all three of Durant's henchmen into motion. The air filled with wildly flying slugs. Slocum slammed hard into the wall and slid down it, trying to keep Matthews in his sights. The burly sailor upended the table and hid behind it. Slocum fired two rounds through the table to flush him out.

Nothing happened.

"In here! Dammit, who let him get in?"

Shotgun blasts made Slocum's ears roar. He got off another shot as one man dived out the window. From the way he jerked, Slocum knew he'd hit him. But he couldn't find Matthews.

"My watch, dammit, where's my watch?" he bellowed. Kicking the table aside, he saw that Matthews had gone through a trap door leading into a cellar. Slocum ducked as hot shotgun pellets roared past his face. He fired through the doorway until his pistol hit an empty cylinder. Without hesitation, he dropped into the cellar.

Darkness engulfed him. Above came the sounds of boots pounding on the floorboards. Slocum knew better than to wait around for them to find the trap door. He was a sitting duck outlined by the light coming from above. Gingerly feeling his way, he edged into the cellar. Every sense straining, he tried to figure out where Matthews had gone.

"There. Down below!" came the cry. A shotgun blast ripped into the dirt floor behind him. Slocum didn't hurry. To stumble and fall meant his death. He found a stone wall and followed it, hoping to find the fleeing British sailor.

A head poked past the rim of the trap door. Slocum's hand closed on the ebony handle of his Colt. He could have blown the fool's head off if his pistol had been loaded. Hunkering down, he fumbled out new ammunition.

"Don't see the son of a bitch, but he's down there someplace."

"Go after him," urged another.

"You go."

While they argued, Slocum reloaded. His eyes adjusted to the dimness, and he continued his hunt for Matthews. When the incautious river man stuck his head back down into the cellar, Slocum snapped off a quick shot. The man sagged; someone above pulled him back.

Slocum wished he could rely on someone to pull him to safety. The men above him started firing through the floor. Splinters cascaded down on his head, mixed with deadly lead slugs.

Frantic now, he sought the door out. However Matthews had left, he had hidden the route behind him. Slocum's nose crinkled when he smelled coal oil. He never thought about the danger as he used the butt of his pistol to knock a hole in the bottle and spray the flammable liquid around the cellar. A single shot ignited it.

The cellar danced with flames. In the glare, Slocum saw the door Matthews had used. He ran to it and kicked it down. The men in the parlor first smelled, then saw the danger. They cried out in fear as they raced from the burning building.

Slocum plunged ahead, the crackling sounds of voracious fire spurring him to ever greater speed. He raced down the narrow dirt-walled passageway and quickly found himself by the outhouse.

Of Zebediah Matthews there was no trace.

Behind him the fire leaped higher and higher. In the distance Slocum heard the fire bells clanging and the firemen beginning their thankless task of getting water into barrels. In a few minutes, a hook and ladder rig with the name PIONEER FIRE COMPANY emblazoned on the side came rattling to a halt. The men piled off the wagon and started work. Several others milled around the perimeter of the fire, unsure what to do. When the flames exploded the bottles of liquor in the back room, some were knocked flat.

Slocum dropped to his knees and examined the

ground for Matthews's trail. He cursed loudly when he found nothing. The ground had been dry for some time; a brief rain shower had turned parts to mud. Tracking in it would be impossible.

He gave up and headed back toward the center of town, his eyes peeled for any sign of the watch-stealing, double-crossing British sailor.

Slocum finally admitted that the man had outfoxed him. Returning to the Headquarters House, he saw that the men still lounged around the front and back doors. They had to be Benjamin Durant's henchmen. He slipped up behind one and stood, unnoticed. The man chewed and spat a gobbet of dark tobacco juice into the street.

"Think he's ever comin' out?" the man asked his partner.

"Why'n the hell should he? He's up there screwing Durant's wife."

"Maybe his daughter, too. They're damned fine-looking fillies. Wouldn't mind gettin' either of them myself."

Slocum drifted away, sure that his absence hadn't been detected. He went up NP Avenue to Rossiter's General Store. With the town being dry, Slocum knew that the best place to find out what he needed was by the store's front door. He almost laughed aloud when he saw three men sitting and sawing away at small bits of wood and gossiping like old women at a quilting bee.

"Howdy," Slocum said, perching on a hitching post in front of the store. The men leaned their chair back against the general store's front, their feet swinging back and forth in the dust. Nowhere in the town had Slocum seen wooden sidewalks.

"You must be the gent who came into town with Durant's daughter." A gimlet-eyed stare appraised him. The man finished and spat, returning to his careful whittling. "Don't see many of your kind in town."

SLOCUM AND THE RED RIVER RENEGADES 139

"What kind is that?"

"Duded up like that, you have to ask?" The one man spoke for the trio. Neither of the others seemed inclined to talk. "Been a real drouth of people through here since the Panic."

"The one a couple years back?"

"When else? Old man Fargo and his NP Railroad went belly up. Still trying to sort through his dealings. Heard tell Hill's trying to buy it all up and merge it into the Great Northern routes."

"The railroad has been good to Fargo, though. Looks to be a bridge going in over the Red River just south of the Moorhead ferry."

"They'll finish it one day. If'n the whole damn town don't burn to the ground first." The man cocked his head to one side. "You wouldn't know nothing about that, now would you?"

"Why do you ask?" Slocum wondered if anything went on in town that this man didn't see or hear.

"Heard tell you was runnin' from the place. One of them booze-and-whore places so popular with the river men."

"The railroad might be in trouble, but the river traffic looks brisk," observed Slocum, trying to swing the man around to what he wanted to hear about most.

"Over in Moorhead they got five steamers, six barges, and eleven flatboats docked right now. That's not counting the ones Durant is building." The man spat again and made a wry face as if the very name put a bad taste in his mouth. "Seems like we can do with a mite less of Durant and a tad more of J. J. Hill."

"You don't like Durant, do you?"

"Ain't many around who do. The bastard's cheap with his wages, high with his shipping, steals most all the lumber for his damned barges, sells bricks for a thief's price, and then there's the..." The old man's voice trailed off.

"The Sioux raiding along the Red River?" prompted Slocum.

"You one of his men?"

Slocum shook his head. "Just helping his wife out. She's here to get a divorce."

"Heard that. Kinsbury soaked her good. Charged a thousand dollars for the divorce. The shyster's gonna need the money once Durant finds out."

"Meaning, Kinsbury will have to run for the hills?"

"Hills? Ain't no hills hereabouts. He's gonna have to leave the flamin' *territory!*"

"What kind of Indian trouble has there been?"

"You keep comin' back to that." The man looked at his two companions. They worked hard on their whittling, as if they heard nothing. Slocum knew that they memorized every word and would repeat it for weeks.

"Seems odd to find Sioux raiding along the river. Times that hard?"

"Worse. Drouth has given us a few bad years of grain. Hard to find water. People livin' in dugouts along the river are almost starvin'. Hard to be an Indian on the reservation, too."

"You're not blaming them for raiding the steamboats, then?"

The man spat and folded his knife before tucking it away in his pants pocket. "Can't say I believe the raids are done by Injuns. Not too hard to figure out why I think that way, though there's some who dispute it." He pointedly looked at his friends. They whittled faster and said nothing.

"Oh?" Slocum was interested in hearing how someone else had come to the same conclusion he had by direct observation of the fake Indians.

"Back in '72, some of the Santee Sioux came ridin' up and camped over in the Oak Grove area. They're about the only ones ever around here and they didn't last but one season."

"That's because Captain Stanley and his troopers came up from Fort Abercrombie and drove 'em away," spoke up one of the silent men. He looked embarrassed at having spoken and dropped his eyes back to his wood carving.

"Ed's right. Bill Stanley was on his way to Fort Abe Lincoln in Bismarck and don't reckon he meant much by the visit, but it drove them away. Seen some travois marks but that might have been from Sioux hightailin' it elsewhere. No reason for them to pick on steamboats in these parts."

"And?" urged Slocum, knowing there was more.

"You figured it out, son. I see it in your eyes. The only steamboats *not* bedeviled by these renegades belong to Benjamin Durant. Don't that strike you as downright peculiar?"

"Goes along with what I saw out on the prairie," said Slocum. "The *City of Moorhead* was attacked and Miss Durant was kidnapped. I got her back, but they were the strangest-looking Sioux I ever came across."

"How strange?" He had the attention of all three men.

"One spoke with a English accent."

"Must be kin to that Matthews fellow," said the talkative old man. His eyes twinkled. "He's about the only Brit in these parts. Most everyone else is Swedish or German."

"Don't think the phony Indian is any kin," said Slocum.

"No, reckon not. Just an old man's wild guess."

"Might be informative to talk to this Zebediah Matthews, though. You wouldn't know where I could find him?"

"Don't remember saying his Christian name. You know that if you have business with him, you probably have business with Durant?"

"You know I'm tangled up with the Durant family

already. But I don't care if Matthews paints himself up like a Sioux warrior and robs paddlewheelers. I'm more interested in getting back what he stole from me."

"Don't know where you could find him now that Durant's illegal saloon and whorehouse burned to the ground. Unless you inquired over at the Red River Barge and Brick Company. Seem to remember both are owned by Durant. Might even catch sight of the likes of Zebediah Matthews."

"Much obliged," said Slocum, jumping down into the dirt.

"Don't go thankin' me none, son. They's rough and tough river men who don't take spit off no one. Even someone as fancy-dressed as you."

"Thanks." The expression on Slocum's face made the old man smile. He and his friends might have more to talk about than the drought before John Slocum left town.

15

Slocum wandered along the river, eyed the drydocks where Durant built the barges and flat-bottomed boats, then turned inland to the brick works. Oily black plumes rose from smokestacks unmistakably marking the factory. Slocum heaved a sigh. What else was there for Fargo besides shipbuilding, farming, and brick-making? In spite of the Red River flowing by so close, there seemed little enough drinking water. The railroad that promised civilization had fallen on hard times. He'd heard that the line shut down entirely in winter and only ran a train a day to Bismarck. He and the ladies had been lucky to reach the spur line from the terminus on the Minnesota River.

He slowed as he neared the brick yard. Men toiled in the hot sun while a supervisor watched them from the shade and drank water from a bottle. Slocum looked around. This was the type of place Zebediah might run.

The Civil War had been fought to free the slaves in the South. Nothing had been done farther north, from the way the Red River Barge and Brick Company treated its workers.

Slocum wiped sweat from his face as he neared the yard. The intense heat from the baking kilns combined with the humid heat along the river to make living almost impossible.

"I ain't seen you before," the supervisor called out. "You got business around here?"

"Looking for a friend of mine. Heard tell he was here."

"Who might that be?" The supervisor strutted over, his belly hanging over a gunbelt straining to hold back the tides of fat. Sandy-haired and pig-eyed, he radiated contempt for the lesser men in the world—which Slocum guessed was damned near everyone else.

"Zeb Matthews. He left so fast I didn't have a chance to give him the money I owe."

"Left?"

"He was over at the scene of the fire, earlier on in the day." Slocum pointed in the direction of the burned-out husk of the illegal saloon. "We gambled a spell and I lost a few dollars. He lit out like the devil was chasing him and I didn't give what he'd won."

"Gimme the money. I'll see that he gets it."

Slocum tried not to smile too broadly. The old man in front of the general store had steered him directly to Matthews. This fat-assed supervisor wanted to steal the money he thought was owed to Matthews. That didn't surprise Slocum. But the supervisor's expression had betrayed knowing Zebediah Matthews.

"I came all the way over from the hotel to give it to him. Might as well see it through. Might be able to talk him into letting me try to win some of it back."

The pig-faced man licked his lips and took another pull on the water in his bottle before answering. "He's over in the yard. The other side of the piles of brick."

"Much obliged." Slocum walked slowly, straining to hear if the supervisor came after him. He expected an ambush. He had seen too many venal men like this to trust them for an instant.

Slocum was so busy worrying about the supervisor's treachery that he almost walked square into Matthews.

"You!" the renegade cried. "Don't you *ever* give up?"

Slocum's hand flashed for his pistol. Matthews

rushed him, strong arms circling Slocum's body and pinning his arms at his sides. The British sailor grunted and heaved, getting Slocum off his feet. Struggling in the bear hug, Slocum felt his strength ebbing.

His back bent as Matthews applied more and more pressure. Biting his lip sent a tiny flood of salty blood down his chin, but the pain brought a surge of strength. Slocum twisted just enough in Matthews's killing grip to get his hand fully on the trigger of his Colt. He fired, not caring what he hit.

Matthews screeched in pain. The pressure on his back suddenly gone, Slocum fell to the ground. He knew he couldn't let the burly sailor attack again. His strength had faded too fast during the first assault. Slocum drew his pistol and aimed it, his hand shaking.

"The watch, you son of a bitch. I want the watch."

Matthews stared at him in disbelief. "That's all? I give you the watch and you walk away?"

"The watch." Slocum's finger tensed on the trigger.

Something about the change in Matthews's attitude warned him. He tried to gun down the sailor—and failed. A heavy wood stake crashed into the back of his skull. Even as he fell face down in the dirt, he knew his bullet had gone wide of its target.

"Who is this son of a mule, Zeb?"

"Don't rightly know, but he's gonna end up fish food in the river. Help me get him down to the banks, mate."

"I ain't your mate. Quit callin' me that."

Matthews made an ugly sound and the two argued for a few seconds. This gave Slocum enough time to regain his wits. The back of his head felt as if he had been kicked by a horse. His back protested every twist and turn he made. The earlier injuries all came back to haunt him. But he moved. Faster than he would have thought possible, he rolled, got to his feet, and ran like a bat out of hell.

"He's gettin' away!" came the cry behind him. Slocum wasn't sure where he ran. Blindly, he stumbled forward, banging into mountains of rough red brick. Reeling, he fell into a dark shed and closed the door behind him.

He lay panting on the dirt floor. From outside came angry shouts and curses. Matthews sought him. Strange plans formed and died in his dazed brain. What would Benjamin Durant do if he learned that his henchman tried to double-cross him? Would Durant even care? His wife getting a divorce might occupy more of his thoughts than turncoat fake Sioux renegades.

Slocum reloaded the spent chambers in his Colt Navy. He knew he would need every shot to get away alive from the brick company.

Touching the bloodied spot on the back of his head made him wince. He stood. For a few seconds, the world spun in crazy circles. Then he steadied. Purpose filled him. He had failed to corner Matthews twice. The third time he would succeed.

He peered out the door and squinted against the bright noonday sun. Men carrying picks and long metal pry bars patrolled the grounds. He tried to hear Matthews's English accent giving orders. Slocum heard only the grumbling of men pushed to the limit of endurance in backbreaking jobs.

He stretched and worked some of the knots from his muscles. He dared not let Matthews get much of a head start on him. The British sailor had proven too slippery for that. When he got his watch back, Zebediah Matthews could go to hell for all he cared. Until Robert's watch rested in his vest pocket where it belonged, Slocum vowed never to give up the hunt.

Several men stalked by outside the shed. Slocum let them go past, then slipped out and trailed them. As they passed the main office, he ducked inside. If Matthews was anywhere to be found, it would be here.

The office was littered with books and invoices for

shipping the tons of brick manufactured by the company. Slocum stopped and stared at one open ledger. He didn't know much about the shipping business, but he knew that it didn't pay to move as little brick as one order showed—and all the way upriver to Winnipeg.

He grinned crookedly. The brick yard might serve as a cover for transporting the booty the fake Indian renegades stole from other steamboat owners. Who questioned shipments of brick? Who in Fargo even cared what Durant did? The man had a license to steal and he used it freely. Not only did he drive competition on the Red River out of business, he feathered his own nest.

How much did Matthews steal for his own use?

"There he is!"

Slocum jerked around and dropped into a crouch. His Colt came up. He fired at the two men fighting to get into the small office. The first bullet struck one in the shoulder. He twisted about and fell face down in the dirt outside. The second man cried out in rage and charged like a bull buffalo.

Slocum's bullet caught him square in the middle of the chest—and it didn't even slow down the mountain of gristle and pure mean. The man's momentum pushed Slocum back into the wall. He grunted and almost blacked out. Matthews had worked him over better than he'd thought. His back threatened to snap at any instant.

The brawny man struck out at Slocum with clumsy blows. Just dodging them put more of a strain on his back than he could stand. Slocum groaned and collapsed to the floor, the man towering over him.

A heavy fist crashed into the side of his head. Dazed, Slocum waited for the second. It never came. He blinked through a veil of red pain and saw that the man had finally died from the gunshot. Slocum pushed the man away and struggled to his feet. He was in no condition to go after Matthews. Fighting his way through an acre of men built like this one didn't appeal to him —not in as much pain as he was.

Slocum got to the door and saw a small knot of the brick-company workers near a kiln. The supervisor harangued them to go look for the intruder. Slocum decided that he wasn't up to facing even the portly supervisor. Retreat galled him when he was this close to Matthews, but he knew he had to leave.

Dead men don't need watches.

Limping and aching with every step, Slocum walked directly away from the gathering crowd of workers. By the time he reached Front Street, the pain had worked out of his body but the wound on the back of his head refused to clot. A steady stream of blood oozed out and trickled down his collar. His new clothing had turned into a bloody morass by the time he got back to the Headquarters House.

He heaved a deep sigh of resignation. Durant's men still patrolled around it, waiting for him to leave. Slocum considered simply going in past them to see what they might do.

He discarded such a notion. They might have orders to gun him down. They could certainly overpower him with little trouble. After the fight in the brick factory, he wasn't sure he could do more than roll over and die. Worst of all, the desk clerk in the hotel would call in the marshal. No guest stumbled through *that* lobby looking like he did and without drawing instant attention and concern.

The setting sun cast long shadows across the prairie by the time Slocum decided to make his move. Sliding along the hotel's northern wall afforded him some cover. The shadows deepened by the time he got to the drain pipe he had slid down earlier in the day. Climbing up proved almost beyond his strength. Slocum collapsed face down on the balcony, panting for breath, when he got to the second floor.

SLOCUM AND THE RED RIVER RENEGADES 149

He lifted his head when he heard movement. At the far end two men sat and stared out across the prairie. The clink of glasses and soft conversation came to him. They imbibed illegal liquor and enjoyed the cooling breezes off the Red River.

Slocum crawled on his belly until he reached the doors leading in to his room. He got inside without the men noticing him. He sank down onto the bed and let out a deep sigh of relief.

"You look a fright, John."

His hand dragged out his Colt. He had it out and cocked before he realized it had been Nicole Durant who spoke.

"You startled me. You shouldn't do that."

"You are mighty quick with your gun," she said, coming to him and sitting on the edge of the bed. He pushed the six-shooter back into its holster and closed his eyes.

The girl's perfume filled his nostrils. All day long he had endured sweat and brick dust and the heavy stench of a city locked in the fiery grip of summer. This gentle fragrance reminded him of happier times, other places. Her soft touch on his forehead told him that everything was right.

"Your new clothing. It's ruined. Cuts and tears and dirt." Nicole touched the spot on the back of his head with her fingertips. Even this brushing contact sent waves of pain through him. Slocum thought the room had turned upside down and threaten to tumble him from the bed.

"There, there," Nicole said, holding him. "There's nothing to be upset about. Not now. Let me clean that nasty wound."

Slocum must have passed out while she worked. When he came to, it had turned to night outside and he was lying naked between cool linen sheets. Warmth stirred next to him.

He sat bolt upright.

"Are you in pain?" Nicole asked. She turned over and stretched. The white sheet moved from her. She lay naked beside him, her breasts creamy mounds in the faint moonlight coming through the open French doors.

"They sit out on the balcony. You shouldn't—" He found his words cut off by her lips pressing into his.

"If we don't make any noise, they won't look in, will they?" Firm hands pushed him flat on the bed. "You aren't disappointed, are you?"

"Disappointed? I'm delighted. But I'm not in much condition to do you any good."

"I don't know, John. This hasn't been injured. See?" She stroked him beneath the sheet. In spite of his throbbing head wound and the pain lingering in the rest of his body, he found himself responding to her slow ministrations.

"Don't reckon there's any hurry, is there?"

"We have all night."

He sighed and enjoyed the nearness of the lovely blonde, her hands doing things that awoke passion in his loins, the coolness of the wind blowing through the open doors.

"Your mother's divorce will be final in the morning?"

"I don't want to talk about it." She rolled over and half lay on his chest. Her lips found the hollow under his ear. She kissed and licked and began nibbling at his earlobe.

"We should," he said. "What are you going to do afterward?"

"When she's no longer Mrs. Benjamin Durant?"

"Exactly."

Nicole fell silent for so long that Slocum thought she had fallen asleep. She finally stirred and moved off him and lay so that her lips were just inches away. Her hot breath gusted in and out of his ear.

"Mama is going back to France."

"What about you?"

"I don't want to go. Not now. She was born on the Continent. This is my home, but Papa would make life unbearable for me." She snuggled closer and buried her face in his shoulder. "He is so awful."

Slocum wrapped his arm around her and held her close. His desire for her died and became something softer, something more protective. He wondered what sort of animal Benjamin Durant was.

16

Slocum awoke with a start. The light slanted through the window and told him that it was far too late to be getting up. He should have checked on Mrs. Durant hours ago. Disengaging his arm from around Nicole, he climbed out of bed. Every bone in his body ached. He stretched and wished he had time for a hot bath.

He looked back at the sleeping girl. He wished he had time for a lot more, too. But he didn't. He quietly put on his clothing, favoring his ribs. He wondered if he would ever feel whole again. The place where he had got hit on the back of the head throbbed constantly. The only bright spot was that it didn't affect his vision. More than once he had been hit in the head and it had caused everything to blur for days.

Checking his Colt and reloading two chambers he found suspect, Slocum felt as ready as he'd ever get to tackle Benjamin Durant head on. If there would be a time when the shipping magnate forced the issue, it would be this morning.

Claudette Durant was going to get her divorce, even if Slocum had to leave a mile of corpses on the way to the courthouse.

"John?" Nicole stirred on the bed. She stretched, her arms going high above her head and exposing her to the waist. Slocum wasn't sure he had ever seen a more beautiful sight.

"Good morning. I didn't mean to wake you."

"You weren't beside me." Her blue eyes came to rest on the Colt he still held in his hand. "There isn't any trouble, is there?"

"Not yet." He slid it into the soft leather holster and tried to smooth the wrinkles in his coat so that he looked more presentable. He didn't do a good job. This outfit, too, had been ruined by his sojourn through the brick yard seeking out Zebediah Matthews. Sooner or later he would have to get a serviceable suit of clothes and forget about looking like a Mississippi river gambler.

"You expect some?"

"Of course I do. Your father didn't strike me as the kind of gent who'd let this rest without raising a ruckus."

"Why can't he let us go?" A tear formed in the corner of her eye. Slocum went and held her, then gently pulled away.

"Get dressed. It's going to be a long morning, unless I miss my guess."

Mrs. Durant gave him and Nicole a long look of disapproval then bustled off ahead of them, going down the wide wood staircase and into the lobby. There two men waited.

From the head of the stairs Slocum spotted them. "Mrs. Durant, get down!" he shouted. Even as the words were leaving his lips, his hand was moving with lightning speed for his Colt Navy. The ebony handle smacked hard into his palm. His fingers curled around the butt and dragged it free. As it came out, he was cocking the hammer. By the time he leveled the six-shooter, his finger was firmly on the trigger—and squeezing.

The report momentarily deafened him. Some quirk in the hotel's construction caused the gunshot to echo around him. But Slocum didn't let this slow him. The muzzle swung about and centered on the second gunman below. The first lay flat on his back, Slocum's bullet in his chest.

"Wait! We can talk this out!" the gunman cried. "I ain't got a feud with you."

"Get him out of here," Slocum said in a cold voice. The gunman's head bobbed like a baited float in a fish-filled pond. He bent over his fallen comrade. As he did so, Slocum fired again.

The fool had tried to pick up the battered cap-and-ball black powder colt Dragoon .44 his dead partner had dropped.

Slocum's bullet missed its mark in the man's head but found flesh in his upper shoulder. He sagged forward, clutching his wound.

"Dammit, I wasn't tryin' nothing."

"Get him the hell out of here."

The gunman started dragging the dead man out with his good arm. By this time, the others in the lobby started to stir and realize that they still lived. Within seconds the marshal came bustling through the broad front doors, a sawed-off shotgun waving about.

"Be careful with that, sir!" Mrs. Durant reached over and pushed the weapon down so that it aimed at the floor. "You might hurt innocent bystanders."

"Never seen a bystander yet who was innocent," the marshal said. "What'n the hell's going on here?"

He looked around the lobby. The small crowd faded away like mist in the morning sun. The marshal cleared his throat and pulled the shotgun barrel away from Claudette Durant.

"You caused quite a stir," he said, shifting his weight from foot to foot. His muddy brown eyes watched Slocum come down the stairs. Slocum made a point of getting his pistol back into its holster. The last thing he needed was an edgy marshal with a scattergun.

"They started it. I saw one getting *that* out." Slocum pointed to the ancient black powder pistol on the floor.

"They were going to kidnap Mrs. Durant and her daughter."

"Heard tell there was some unpleasantness. That's why I was on my way over." The marshal scratched his stubby chin, making his thick mustache twitch. "You folks are puttin' me in a bad situation."

"Mrs. Durant..." Slocum started. The marshal silenced him with a wave of his hand.

"I know all about due process, mister. That's what makes it so bad for me. The lady's got every right to get her divorce from Mr. Durant. Fact is, Benjamin Durant is a powerful man. He owns the brick factory and the barge docks and ships damned near everything into town. Come harvest season, most all the grain is shipped upriver on his steamboats. He's a *real* powerful man in these here parts."

"The law, Marshal."

"Don't go spoutin' the law to me, son. I know it better'n you, 'less I miss my guess. But I'm caught on the horns of a dilemma."

Slocum let the man work his way through the problem of upholding the law and Claudette's right to a divorce and appeasing a rich and powerful pillar of society in Fargo. The play of shadow and thought on his face told Slocum what he needed to know. The marshal was an honorable man and would do the right thing, even if it landed him in a peck of trouble.

"Let's get on down to the courthouse. Mr. Kinsbury is probably chewing nails and spittin' tacks by now. Never seen a man who was more of a doer and less of a waiter. No patience at all, no sir."

Slocum walked to one side, Nicole close by. The girl wanted to speak but saw he was too intent on watching windows and trying to find some sign that her father wasn't going to cave in easily. They reached the two-story brick courthouse on First Avenue between Seventh and Eighth Streets South before Durant's walrus mustache and the growling mouth behind it put in an appearance.

"There she is. Good work, Marshal Haggart. I'll see you get a nice reward for rescuing her from this ruffian." Durant's mustache tips wiggled as he stared angrily at Slocum.

"There's some small problem here, Mr. Durant. Way I see it, this lady's just exercisin' her rights as a citizen to get a divorce. Stand aside, sir."

"What!" The shock rolled down the street and echoed along every alley in Fargo. Durant staggered back as if he had been struck. His nose had been bandaged from the previous fight with Slocum, and a spot of plaster covered a scrape on his cheek.

"Judge Shannon is gonna have to rule on the merits of her case. I reckon if you got a lawyer, you can plead your side of the matter."

"*My side!* The indignation and rage locked within the man's corpulent body erupted. He darted forward with a speed surprising for one of his bulk and grabbed Claudette. Durant swung her around so hard she smashed into a wall and let out a single sob before sliding down to a heap on the floor.

Slocum was already in motion. His pistol slipped free and centered on the river man nearest Durant. The man froze when he saw the cold eyes and steady hand behind the Colt. To Slocum's surprise, Marshal Haggart acted with as much speed and determination as he had.

The marshal's sawed-off shotgun flashed through the air and collided with the side of Durant's head. The hollow *clunk!* as the metal struck skull was drowned out by the howl of pain as Durant jerked away. A thin river of blood ran down the shipping magnate's head.

"You're damn lucky I didn't blow your fool head off, Mr. Durant," said Haggart. "Reckon I would have, 'cept you're such a prominent man hereabouts."

"I'll have your badge for this, Haggart. I'll have your *life!*"

"More'n one's tried to do both, Durant. Don't expect you'll be the last to try, neither."

Marshal Haggart shoved Durant to one side and helped Claudette to her feet. Supported by the marshal, the woman walked into the courtroom on shaky legs. Slocum followed, his Colt never leaving the men gathered around Benjamin Durant.

They backed away. Slocum swung around and entered, eyes alert for trouble. He frowned. Something struck him as wrong.

"Mrs. Durant, are you all right?" he asked.

"Fine, sir. Thank you for your efforts on my behalf." The icy blonde heaved a deep sigh, and Slocum saw the first glimmerings of real emotion in her. "I will be very glad to have this behind me. When will Judge Shannon arrive?"

"Don't know about the judge," said Marshal Haggart, "but here comes your lawyer."

Striding briskly into the room came the lawyer Kinsbury. The man's face was flushed and he panted as if he had run a country mile.

"You, there, Marshal!" Kinsbury called out, waving his hand. "You've got to do something about those ruffians. They tried to stop me outside the courthouse. How can justice be served if we are all in fear of our lives?"

"The prices you charge your clients, little wonder you're in dread of 'em," muttered Haggart. Louder, the town marshal said, "I'll see to it. Might have a couple of my deputies roust 'em a tad to let 'em know who's in charge around these parts."

The commotion had done nothing to settle Slocum's uneasiness. He sat down just behind a wooden railing dividing the litigants and lawyers from the audience.

Glancing around the room did nothing to allay his gut feeling of something being very wrong.

"Nicole!"

"What's that, Mr. Slocum? What about my daughter?" Claudette Durant dabbed sweat from her face with a lace handkerchief. Even though it was still early morning, the heat inside the courtroom grew to a stifling level.

"Where is she?" Slocum shot to his feet and quickly scanned every shadowy corner of the room. Nicole was nowhere to be seen.

"I don't know. She..." Claudette's voice trailed off when her husband strutted into the courtroom. He pushed through the gate in the wooden railing and motioned both Marshal Haggart and Kinsbury to one side.

"I'd like to speak to her in private."

"Don't go makin' any threats, Mr. Durant," the marshal warned. "I'm takin' a big dislike to the way you're conductin' your end of this business."

Durant's walrus mustache seemed to roll on his upper lip as he sneered. He swung his bulk around and interposed himself between the marshal and Claudette. Slocum was close enough to hear what the man said.

It sent him flying from the courthouse.

Durant had threatened his wife with Nicole's death. Slocum cursed his own stupidity for not checking to be sure the girl was with them when they entered the courthouse. One of Durant's river men had nabbed her and cut her out as slick as any cowpuncher working a herd.

Slocum burst into the bright sunlight and looked both ways up and down First Avenue. Fargo stirred for another day's business in the humidity and hot sun, but of Nicole and her captors he saw no trace. He knew better than to stand and waste time swearing at his own stupidity. She had been kidnapped once by Durant's fake Sioux Indians in an attempt to deter Mrs. Durant from getting a divorce. He hadn't thought they would try it a second time.

Rushing back into the courthouse, he slammed through the low gate and grabbed Durant's cravat. He lifted, the muscles in his arm straining as he heaved the man's bulk up to tiptoe.

"Where is she?"

"Order in the court. What's the meaning of this? Marshal Haggart, eject this man immediately or I'll toss him in the calaboose for a week!"

Slocum glanced over his shoulder. Judge Peter Shannon had already begun the divorce proceedings. From all that Slocum had heard, it was only a formality and Claudette would have her divorce granted within minutes.

The expression on her face told Slocum another story. She wasn't happy. She held back tears and clutched at Kinsbury's sleeve. The dapper lawyer tried to keep her from wrinkling his expensive jacket. He failed.

Slocum released his grip on the shipping magnate and swung to face Haggart. "He had his own daughter kidnapped. His henchmen have Nicole!"

"Don't get so riled, mister." Haggart took Slocum by the arm and steered him from the courtroom. "We're in the middle of a small dilemma. Seems the lady wants to stop the proceedings."

"You can't let her."

"Struck me as odd that she didn't haggle when Mr. Kinsbury said he was keeping her thousand-dollar fee, divorce or no. That doesn't seem like a rational decision on the lady's part, rich or poor." Haggart smiled and shook his head. "The rich folks tend to be tighter with their money than the poor. Reckon as how that's how they got it in the first place."

"What's going to happen?"

"Seems to be a bit of a discussion going on about that," said the marshal.

Slocum jerked free and went to Claudette Durant. "He kidnapped Nicole. Give me an hour and I'll get her back again."

"Mr. Slocum, my husband warned me that I must stop these proceedings."

"That's extortion, ma'am," cut in the lawyer. "We can bring him up on charges for it."

"Shut up." Slocum had no time for legal niceties. Nicole's life hung on the decision they made in the next few minutes. Slocum had no doubt that a man like Durant would kill his own child rather than let his wife get a divorce.

"Why not ask for a short continuance?" asked Haggart. "People do it all the time." He looked toward the bench and Judge Shannon. The man shifted uneasily on the hard seat. "The judge is a might thirsty man, if you catch my meaning."

"Judge Shannon," spoke up Kinsbury, "there seems to be a... legal problem I am presently unprepared to answer with the proper attention to detail. I ask for a one-hour recess to study this matter so that I can better represent my client."

"Make it two hours, fool," grumbled Haggart. He shook his head in disgust. Slocum saw that the town marshal had as little time for lawyers as he did.

"One hour. And we'll finish this matter once and for all time," declared Shannon.

"Your Honor, wait!" Durant tried to stop the judge but the man had already left the courtroom in a swirl of his black judicial robe. The clink of a bottle and the sound of gurgling came from the chamber immediately off the main room. Durant stopped, knowing better than to interrupt the judge in the midst of a drinking spree.

"You won't get away with this," he snarled at Slocum. "My wife is going to remain my property—and you're going to be buried in the potter's field outside town."

"Don't go threatening the boy now, Mr. Durant. Such words don't become a rich and powerful man like you." Marshal Haggart stroked the barrel of his shotgun, emphasizing his gentle order.

"I'll deal with you when this sordid affair is over, Haggart." Durant shoved past them and stormed out of the courthouse.

"Where do you suppose he got off to with his daughter?" asked the marshal.

Slocum had an idea. "Let's try the brick company. There are enough empty sheds to hide an army."

"Always thought that myself," said Haggart. "Somehow, it was never a comforting thought."

Slocum left Mrs. Durant in her lawyer's care and hurried out with the marshal. They might have a small war to fight before they found Nicole. After that, it would get even bloodier. Benjamin Durant was not a man to give up easily.

17

"Why are you doing this, Marshal? Looks to be easier for you to simply say it's none of your business. Benjamin Durant is a powerful man."

"Might cost me my job," Haggart agreed. "I worked damned hard to get elected back in April. But then, it ain't much of a job, and losin' it wouldn't be *that* bad." He smiled broadly. "There's not many in Fargo who much like Durant and that pack of river rats he calls his crew. He throws his weight around too much for most folks. And he's got a considerable amount to throw around, too."

Slocum found himself liking the graying, portly sheriff.

Haggart cocked his head to one side and looked at Slocum from the side of his eye. "Have I ever seen a wanted poster out for you?"

"Never broken the law in the Dakotas," Slocum said honestly. He had no idea what Haggart might have seen on him. His life hadn't been lily-white and pure as the wind-driven snow. And, truth to tell, Slocum had found himself in a world of trouble, not all of it his fault.

"You dress like one of them fancy-ass gamblers, but you don't use that six-shooter like one."

"Nicole Durant's the problem needing a solution, Marshal, not me."

"So you say." The marshal hitched up his belt and checked both chambers of the scattergun. Slocum was glad Haggart's attention had turned back to the kidnapping. He'd hate to gun down the man for getting too curious about an ill-spent past.

"The brick company is about all that's thriving in Fargo, unless you want to count Durant's barge-building dock down on the river. The Panic's still got the railroad officials spooked about the entire region, and the renegades are holding back river travel other'n Durant's."

Marshal Haggart stopped and held out his hand to prevent Slocum from charging directly into the brick yards.

"Suppose I ought to rustle up a couple deputies, but there don't seem to be time for that. You think we can do this chore all by ourselves?" Haggart saw the set of Slocum's chin and laughed. "Hell, you look like you could do it all by your lonesome. Maybe I should get my ass on back to the office and rest these old bones."

"Do as you please, Marshal."

"Just a joke, son. Don't take things so personal. They'll sneak up on you and bite you on the rear." Haggart studied the empty field stretching in front of them. Piles of brick stood everywhere, giving a sniper inside tremendous advantage. The only vegetation in sight were a few bright green clumps of Russian thistle. "Surely is quiet. Don't think Durant gave 'em the day off. He's too cheap, the bastard."

Slocum wondered what stuck in Haggart's craw about Durant. It didn't pay to ask. He'd accept the lawman's help in getting Nicole back and that would end it.

At least, he hoped that would see the last of Benjamin Durant. Slocum's belly began to knot up at the idea the shipping magnate would really harm his own daughter. From the hints Nicole had given, Durant had done as much as he possibly could to her over the years. Slocum's hand tightened on the ebony butt of his Colt as he thought of the girl with her father.

"You're really takin' this to heart, aren't you?" asked

Haggart. "You thinking to go off with that frisky little filly when the shooting's over and done?"

"Hadn't thought about it," Slocum lied. He had. The idea of being with Nicole seemed better and better.

"You surely do make it hard for yourself. Even with that fine suit of clothes, you ain't within a mile of her society. I can tell. Some rich folks come through town now and again. I watch 'em and wonder what makes 'em tick. Never figured it out. But they're different, you bet." Haggart looked sideways at Slocum. "Me and you got a lot in common, though."

Slocum knew what Haggart was trying to tell him, in his roundabout fashion. He and the marshal were of a kind—and he and Nicole were not. Deep down, Slocum knew the truth but shoved it away. He had to get her back before he made any of the hard decisions.

"Lookin' as if I made a big mistake," said Haggart. The man fumbled in his shirt pocket and pulled out a plug of chewing tobacco. He silently offered it to Slocum, who refused. The marshal took a big bite and tucked the remainder away in his pocket as he began chewing. Only after he spat did he continue. "Should fetch a deputy or two for this." He grinned broadly. "But why share the fun?"

With that he pointed to his left, indicating the direction Slocum should go. The marshal pulled back the hammers on his scattergun and started to the right.

Slocum started, got a few yards, then stopped. Everything felt wrong. He carefully studied the mounds of bricks around him waiting for shipment and saw nothing. Straining, all he heard was the soft, hot wind whistling through the stacks. He had no sense of another living being around.

Backtracking, he followed Marshal Haggart. He made damned sure that the marshal didn't spin and use both barrels on him, but the gut-level feeling he depended on so much told him this was right.

A fusillade of different-caliber shots rang out. Tiny pops of small-bore guns and the bull-throated roar of a shotgun discharging filled the air. Slocum advanced cautiously. He didn't want to find himself on the receiving end of all that flying lead.

Bits of brick flew into the air as the slugs smashed into a small mound not ten feet away. Haggart lay on his belly, cursing, spitting, and trying to reload his shotgun. The gunfire pinned him down effectively. Slocum saw no fewer than six of Durant's henchmen with rifles and six-shooters moving through the mountains of straw, clay, and finished red bricks.

"You hit?" Slocum shouted.

"Naw. It takes more than those owlhoots to get me. But I did swallow my chew," the marshal said, his eyes never leaving the stack of bricks where the nearest two bushwhackers crouched. Haggart rose up just as one man poked his head around the shielding bricks. The shotgun's roar drowned out the man's scream of pain.

Slocum winced. The scream died in an ugly gurgle. Haggart had blown away most of the man's head from the nose up. The man's partner swung a Winchester around and got off a quick shot at the marshal. Slocum didn't let him get in a second shot.

The Colt barked once. The man sagged, his hands clutching at the slowly blossoming red rose staining his upper chest. Slocum saw the accuracy of his shot and moved on immediately. He and the lawman were still outnumbered—and he had to find Nicole. Durant was not above using his daughter as a shield to escape.

"There are still four of 'em left," called Haggart.

Slocum didn't respond. He knew the men facing them would home in on his voice just like a carrier pigeon. Bent double, he ran past the marshal and dived flat on his belly and came to rest behind a low handcart used to move bricks. From this vantage, he saw two men with rifles working their way toward the marshal.

Both of Slocum's shots found their targets, but from the screams and curses he knew neither had been a clean hit. The men sported wounds, nothing serious. This made them even more dangerous than before.

Slocum left the wounded pair for Haggart and wriggled on his stomach through the dust until he came to a shed. He pulled himself upright and looked through a dirty window. The shed was empty. Using the butt of his pistol, he knocked out the window and used the sill as a step to get up to the low roof. He squirmed and kicked and got onto the dusty shingled roof. Prone, he lay in wait for the men remaining in the brick yard. The days he had spent as a sniper during the War came rushing back to him. He had been one of the Confederacy's best. With a captured Yankee Sharps, he'd lie on a hilltop and wait for sunlight to glint off an officer's braid. Kill the head and the body died.

It worked well with men and armies. No officers, poor performance in battle. Slocum had several shots at Durant's hired gunmen that he passed up. He wanted Benjamin Durant.

The roar of Haggart's shotgun filled his ears. Slocum still didn't move a muscle. He had learned patience during the War. That separated him from so many others. And it kept him alive.

The marshal charged around like a head-maddened bull. The owlhoots hunting him fell into his trap. And still Slocum waited for a glimpse of Durant. If the man had brought his daughter to the brick factory, he had to be flushed out soon by Haggart.

Slocum sweated gallons in the hot Fargo sun. His skin wrinkled and burned and threatened to peel off his body. He did not move a muscle. The sweat ran into his eyes and burned. He allowed himself a quick swipe to keep his vision clear.

"Where'n the hell are you, Slocum?" Marshal Haggart had finished off the shipping magnate's hired guns. "You didn't catch a slug between the eyes, now did you? You didn't look to be the careless type. Where are you?"

Slocum let Haggart wander away from the shed where he kept his vigil. The sun seemed to grow even more intense. For an instant Slocum thought he watched a mirage dancing out of the corner of his eye. Turning slightly, he saw Durant dragging Nicole from a shed that might have been the duplicate of the one on which he lay in wait.

He moved carefully, not wanting to draw attention to his position. He wished he had his old sniper's rifle. With a handgun the shot was difficult.

He tried anyway, even if it endangered Nicole. Slocum figured that she was in less danger from his marksmanship than she was from her father.

The Colt Navy bucked. He cocked it again and fired a second time. Benjamin Durant shouted something he couldn't make out, but Slocum saw that he had not stopped the man. He had erred on the side of caution, his shots going wide to avoid the struggling Nicole.

Slocum slid down the sloping roof, caught the edge with his left, and tumbled over. He dangled for an instant, then dropped into a crouch, his six-shooter ready to take on Durant.

"He's hightailin' it for the river," came the marshal's cold words. "You plumb missed him. Surprised the hell out of me, too."

"We've got to stop him before he reaches a steamboat. If he gets on one, he'll be out of our reach."

"It's not quite that easy, son," Marshal Haggart assured him. "Takes more than a rich man's whim to get a paddlewheeler going along the river."

Slocum barely listened. He dropped to one knee and worked to reload his Colt. He wished he had brought his other pistol with him. That oversight gave Durant a greater head start than he deserved. Only when his six-shooter was loaded and ready again, though, did Slocum go after Durant. He wanted a full six shots for the shipping magnate.

"This here road winds around and goes down to the barges and the dry dock," said Haggart. "I figure Durant is heading there. Might be able to hide out on one of the barges until he can get away."

Ahead Slocum saw the flash of yellow off Nicole's dress. The girl fought hard to keep from going along with her father. This slowed him enough that the marshal got into position above and aimed the shotgun straight at Durant.

"You thinkin' on leavin' Fargo, Mr. Durant?" the marshal asked in a deceptively quiet voice. He peered down the double barrels of the sawed-off shotgun, as if this accomplished anything. They all knew he need only point the scattergun in the general direction of his target to hit it. Hot lead pellets would explode in a wide and uncontrolled cone.

Slocum moved quickly to get into position, too. He preferred using his more accurate pistol. If Haggart cut loose, Nicole would be seriously hurt—or killed.

"This is a family dispute, Haggart. It's none of your concern."

"I'm makin' it mine, I reckon," the marshal said. The cocking of both hammers sounded like the pealing of a death bell. This took the starch out of Benjamin Durant real quick.

He released Nicole. She stumbled and fell, then got to her feet and ran to Slocum. He caught her around the waist and spun the girl around so his body shielded her. Durant had a six-shooter in one hand. The barrel rose slightly, as if he considered shooting both Slocum and his daughter. Then he gave up. Durant shoved the pistol into his waistband.

"This is an outrage, Marshal. I'll have your badge for it."

"Let's just mosey on back into town. By now, I reckon your wife is your former wife." Durant's anger seemed to please Haggart. Slocum just wanted it to be at an end.

"Oh, John," sobbed Nicole. She buried her face in his shoulder. He felt hot, wet tears soaking into his shirt. "He threatened me. Even worse than before. The things he said he'd do. The man's a monster!"

"He can't hurt you now."

"I'm going to throw him in jail for a spell," said Haggart, herding Durant around with the muzzle of his shotgun so that he could pull the man's pistol from his belt.

"You can't do that!" protested Durant.

"Can and will. Don't figure I got enough to put you in permanent-like, but I can make sure you don't annoy these fine ladies no more."

"Haggart—"

"None of that, Mr. Durant." The marshal put special emphasis on the "mister." Again Slocum wondered what the lawman had against Durant. Whatever it was, it stirred powerful emotions in Haggart.

"Let's get back to the courthouse and see about your mother," said Slocum. He guided Nicole away from her father. Marshal Haggart touched the rim of his battered brown hat to her as they walked past.

"See you folks later, after I put this gentleman behind bars. I want to make sure you don't have any problems getting out of Fargo. You've caused about as much excitement as this old heart can stand."

"The ladies will be on the next steamboat out," Slocum promised.

"But, John, what about—"

Slocum silenced her. He couldn't forget that he had other business to tend to before he could ever consider leaving. Zebediah Matthews still carried a watch that didn't belong to him.

18

Nicole Durant held his hand so tightly that Slocum thought the circulation began to die. When needles of sensation danced up and down his wrist, Slocum pulled free of her grip. She reluctantly abandoned his hand in favor of pressing her hip against his. Slocum was acutely aware that both the lawyer Kinsbury and Judge Shannon noticed. The looks the two men exchanged went unnoticed by Claudette, however.

"Your hour is up, Mr. Kinsbury," said the judge. "Are you ready to finish the presentation on this divorce hearing?"

"Yes, Your Honor. The plaintiff moves that the divorce be granted immediately."

Judge Shannon stared at the lawyer, then bent forward slightly and asked, "Is *that* the extent of your unforeseen problem with the law, Counselor?"

"Uh, yes, Your Honor."

"I do not see Mr. Durant in court. Is he represented by a lawyer?" Judge Shannon looked around just as John Haggart came into the courtroom. "Marshal, do you know the whereabouts of Mr. Durant?"

"Your Honor, I've got him doing some time in the lock-up."

"On what charge?"

"Disturbin' the peace."

"You make it sound like you're asking me a question

rather than answering mine. Is Mr. Durant formally charged with this crime?"

"Not exactly, Your Honor. There was a little unpleasantness out at the brick factory, and I thought all parties needed time to cool off a mite."

"So a pillar of the Fargo community is in jail and unable to answer the lawsuit before this court?"

"If you mean the divorce, I reckon that's so."

Judge Shannon heaved a deep sigh. "This is highly irregular. Usually, we don't have two parties to contend with. One side comes in and files, the fees are paid, the divorce is granted, and the marriage is ended. A contested divorce is another matter."

"Your Honor, we have no wish to take up more of the court's time. Grant the divorce, and Mrs. Durant will be on her way at the earliest possible moment."

"How early?" asked the judge.

"There's a paddlewheeler at the docks getting ready to leave within the hour for Winnipeg," Kinsbury said. "Mrs. Durant has every intention to be on it, with her daughter."

"Marshal, the court finds you in contempt—unless you release Mr. Durant from jail."

"How long I got to obey, Your Honor?"

Judge Shannon smiled. Slocum realized there were damned few people in Fargo who much liked Durant. "You have two hours to release the prisoner. That ought to satisfy everyone in this courtroom."

"Then the divorce is granted?" Claudette Durant rose and stared at the judge, as if she couldn't believe her ears.

"As long as court fees are paid, I so rule. Next case!" Judge Shannon banged his gavel, saw no new cases, and reached under the bench and came out with a half-filled whiskey bottle. "Anyone want a pull before we get on with it?"

Claudette sagged back into her chair. Slocum had expected tears. She simply stared straight ahead, as if she couldn't believe her ordeal was over. Slocum knew it had just begun unless she got beyond her former husband's long reach.

"What's up in Winnipeg?" he asked her. Nicole pressed close beside him. He realized he would have to make a decision soon.

"Passage for France. I cannot stay in America. Not after today."

Slocum started to ask the obvious, if Nicole was accompanying her mother. Nicole spoke first. "Come with us, John. Please!"

This rocked him back. He had been wondering if she would stay with him. He had no reason to go to Europe.

Everything Marshal Haggart had said came rushing to him. "I don't think so," he answered slowly. "That's not my kind of place. Nobody'd speak so's I could understand them."

"We can be together," urged Nicole. For the first time, Claudette understood. She stared at her daughter in horror for making such a suggestion.

"I've still got unfinished business here," he said, again sidestepping the need to make a decision. "You go get ready to sail to Winnipeg."

"He'll be out soon. The judge ordered him released. We dare not stay." Claudette's mind began to work on other matters now. Slocum saw that she had no intention of allowing her daughter to remain with a crude, unsophisticated American. Worst of all, in her eyes, he was nothing more than a hired hand. He read all that and more in a flash.

"The *City of Moorhead* is the boat that's leaving," said Marshal Haggart. "Let me escort you ladies to your hotel and down to the docks."

"John, wait, please. Let's not—" Nicole was cut off by her mother's insistent pull on her arm. The girl blew him a kiss. Then they vanished out the front door with the marshal between them.

Slocum sagged. He still hadn't made up his mind what to do about Nicole. She obviously desired him, but how long would this last? She had been raised with considerable money and education. In France the girl's sophistication would be required. His own rough manner and lack of formal education would embarrass Nicole—and himself.

Slocum pushed it away. He didn't have to go to France with Claudette. Nicole didn't have to go, either. Not if he took care of her father and his henchman once and for all. Slocum's hand brushed over his Colt's handle. In the fray at the brick yard he had not seen Matthews. The man had to be nearby. If he wasn't Durant's right-hand man, he was certainly a valued assistant.

Slocum smiled crookedly. Left alone, Matthews would end up killing Durant—or the other way around. When the double-cross became apparent and the fake Sioux renegades were exposed for what they were, the entire lot of them would be dead or in jail.

An idea slowly formed. Durant's phony raiders had plagued Fargo and the other shipping companies supplying the town for some time. Not only would turning the owlhoots over to the marshal solve a passel of his problems, it might also earn him a reward.

Slocum hurried toward the Fargo jail, his mind turning over a dozen different ways to get Durant to tell him where to find Matthews. He didn't think the shipping magnate would believe him if he told of Matthews's intention to double-cross him. Durant wasn't likely to believe anything Slocum had to say.

There were other ways of making him talk. Slocum's hands tightened into fists as he considered which ones might be most effective—and which might give him the most satisfaction. He had broken the man's nose. He might start breaking important bones.

Time worked against him. The *City of Moorhead* left within the hour. Haggart had another hour after that to release his prisoner. This left Slocum very little time to squeeze the information he needed from the man.

Slocum barreled into the small jail. A deputy who had been sleeping with his feet hiked up on the desk came awake with a start. "What you wantin'?" he asked with ill-concealed ire at being disturbed from his afternoon nap.

"Want to talk to your prisoner."

"Which one? We got a pair of 'em back there."

"Durant."

"Oh, that pain in the butt. Reckon it's all right. Marshal Haggart didn't say to hold him without talkin' to anyone." The deputy got to his feet, fumbled with a large ring of keys, and opened an iron door leading back into the small cellblock.

"Son of a bitch!" the deputy shouted as he swung the door open.

Slocum pushed past, hand on his Colt Navy. It wasn't needed. The three cells were empty.

"Where'd that son of a bitch go?" the deputy wondered.

Slocum stared into the still-locked cell and saw what the deputy had failed to. The bars in the window had been pulled out and then replaced to give the impression of security to anyone casually glancing into the cell.

"Looks as if you've had a jailbreak. Better find Marshal Haggart and tell him about it."

"Why'd they take that good-for-nothing Len Dyer along with 'em?"

"What was he in for?" asked Slocum, thinking the man might be one of the fake renegades.

"Vagrancy and public drunkenness. Can't keep him sober, no matter what laws we pass. And him the brother of the pastor over at the Lutheran church."

Slocum decided quickly that Matthews—or whoever

had broken Durant out—had detached the bars in Dyer's cell, then realized their mistake. They had let the man go free rather than let him stay behind and identify them, or raise an immediate hue and cry.

Rushing outside, Slocum went around the building and found bits of shredded rope. Horses had been used to pull the bars out of the wall. Slocum found himself picturing the corpulent Benjamin Durant puffing and panting as he wiggled through the small window.

"This marks a first, and one I'd as soon have never recorded against me," came John Haggart's voice. Slocum looked around. The marshal and two deputies stood at the corner of the building. "Having a jailbreak makes you look like a damned fool in the eyes of voters." He scowled at his deputies. The one who had been sleeping in the front office paled under the scrutiny.

Haggart snorted. "You got any idea where these yahoos might have got off to?"

"I know where they took Nicole when they kidnapped her off the *City of Moorhead*."

"Been thinking on that. Never had a report filed, but the captain mentioned Sioux renegades. You sayin' the Injuns might be somethin' else?"

"You hinted at it yourself, Marshal."

"Not much of a secret, except to most folks." Haggart looked disgusted. "Couldn't convince them it wasn't Sioux who wandered off the reservation. Feathers and a bit of war paint fool most of these people every time."

"Didn't anyone notice only Durant's riverboats were immune from attack?"

"Durant owns a newspaper. They print what he tells 'em. The *Fargo Times* does its best to print the truth, but it don't get read by too many folks yet."

"If we get on out to the spot where they camped after kidnapping Nicole off the steamboat, we might catch them."

"You got a stake in this I don't see. Your lady love is all free to go anywhere she pleases. Such a purty blonde lady don't look vindictive to me."

"I've got business with Zebediah Matthews."

"That's all you're gonna say?"

"They might be out of Cass county and into Minnesota if you wait too long to go after them, Marshal."

"Yes, sir, you do have a way about you. Might be you got a *lot* to hide."

"The fake renegades. Durant. Jailbreak. What'll it be, Marshal? All that or idle speculation about me and my motives?"

"Lars, get the horses. Olaf, you're in charge. If we aren't back in a couple days, get up a posse and pull our fat out of the fire." With that, Haggart took care of his administrative duties and got ready to pursue Ben Durant.

By the time Slocum fetched his horse and got back, the marshal and his deputy had packed enough ammunition into their saddlebags to fight a small war.

"Never think your quarry can't outgun you," philosophized Haggart.

Slocum wheeled his horse around and set off at a quick walk. He itched to whip the horse into a gallop, but he knew the distance to the campsite just off the Red River was a good half day's ride. He and Nicole had taken longer, since they had wanted to avoid Matthews and his fake Indian warriors.

As they rode, Haggart pulled up alongside Slocum and asked, "Where exactly along the river did they have their camp? The way we're heading might be the long way."

Slocum described the terrain and country along the Red River the best he could.

"That direction. We go over the hill and down a ravine and see if we can't pick up their trail straight out. Let's hope they're returning to the scene of their crime."

Haggart smiled almost shyly. "I read that in a penny dreadful that came out on the train from St. Paul."

"Marshal," called the deputy. "Here're fresh hoof prints. At least four horses."

Haggart dropped down and hitched up his gunbelt before examining the tracks. Slocum admired the man's technique for studying the spoor and felt happy that he wasn't the one being hunted down. John Haggart looked to be a formidable tracker.

"They're not far ahead of us. The trail's not more than twenty minutes old. See how the Russian thistle is still oozing sap? That shit dries up fast in this heat. Give it an hour and it'd be turning brown and getting ready to die."

Slocum had remained on his horse. He turned his right ear in the direction taken by Durant. Faint sounds came over the small rise.

"We might not be that far behind them. Listen."

"I hear 'em," cried Lars. "Can't be but a hundred yards distant."

"Hush up, boy. Don't go spookin 'em none," cautioned the marshal. He turned to Slocum and said, "We do this according to the law. You're a deputy marshal until I say otherwise."

"No. I won't let you deputize me."

"You don't have a say-so, son. This way, I can hang you if'n you do anything stupid, like shootin' down unarmed prisoners." Haggart spat and worked out a new chew from his plug of tobacco. "Course, you can do any damned thing you please long as they're armed."

Slocum stirred uneasily. He heard the sounds of loud arguments coming from over the rise—he refused to call this pimple on the landscape a hill. He didn't want anything to happen until he got there.

"Let 'em kill each other, son. Remember that. Makes life a bunch easier."

The cold look Slocum shot the marshal told him that

Slocum never took the easy way out. He wanted blood—and he'd get it.

"All right, be like that. Lars, you ready?"

"Ready as rain, Marshal." He held up his Winchester to prove it.

Slocum urged his horse forward, walking her slowly to avoid any surprises. He didn't know exactly where Durant and his henchmen were and he didn't want to overrun their position.

"There's the trail, son." Haggart pointed out the tracks in the dry ground. For all the humidity in the air, Slocum wondered how it could be so dry and hot. Sweat ran down his sides and soaked his clothing.

He stood up in his stirrups for added height. He caught sight of a horse head just over the top of the rise. With a quick motion, he drew his six-shooter and got ready for action.

Haggart motioned. The three rode forward and came to the top of the hill. In a draw around a small pond of water stood Durant, Matthews, and two others. All four saw Slocum and the lawmen at the same time.

Lars fired without hesitation. With surprising accuracy, he knocked the leg out from under one man. Haggart's shotgun roared and sent hot lead pellets winging down among the three standing men. At this range all he did was spook their horses. That proved good enough. Durant dived to catch the reins of his bucking horse and missed. The shipping magnate flopped on his face and struggled to get back up.

"I'll blow your damnfool head off, if you try," came Haggart's cold words. A second blast from his scattergun convinced Benjamin Durant. The man stood, hands held high.

The fourth man tried to get out his pistol from where he had it tucked into his waistband. Slocum fired and missed, cocked and fired a second time before the man unlimbered his pistol. Slocum's third shot ended the frantic attempt. The river man snapped upright, then fell like tall timber sawed through at the base.

Matthews knew better than to fight—he ran.

"I'll get him. He's the one I wanted, anyway," Slocum shouted over his shoulder.

"Be my guest," Haggart said, shaking his head. The stout marshal put his heels gently into his horse's flanks and slowly went down the incline. He had evidence enough for a dozen crimes.

Evidence wasn't what Slocum sought. He wanted his brother's watch back from Matthews. Slocum spurred his horse into a trot to catch up with the fleeing man.

Matthews looked back over his shoulder, saw Slocum riding him down, and abruptly changed his direction. Slocum's horse had been trained to cut calves from a herd. It dodged to block Matthews. The burly British sailor roared and reached for the brace of pistols stuck into his belt.

Slocum never hesitated as he raced by. He kicked free of his stirrups and dropped on top of Matthews with both feet. One boot hit the man in the side of the head and sent him to the ground. Slocum recovered and got to his feet, cascades of dust falling from him. He brought his Colt up and pointed it at Matthews, only to find that the Englishman had one of his own pistols out and aimed.

"This is a Mexican standoff," said Matthews.

"I want my watch back. The one you stole in St. Louis."

"You are a single-minded bloke, ain't you?"

"The watch."

Matthews shifted slightly. He looked back in the direction of Marshal Haggart and his deputy as if judging his chances. They looked better with Slocum.

"Let me go, and I'll give you back the watch, mate."

Slocum saw it dangling from a chain in the man's vest pocket. He shook his head and said, "No deals.

You give me the watch or I'll blow your damned head off."

"We both got pistols on each other."

Slocum said nothing. His cold green eyes locked on the sailor's. Neither man flinched or looked away. To have done so would have spelled instant death.

Slowly, Matthews stuck his pistol back into his belt. He waited for Slocum to do the same.

"Goodbye, mate."

Both men's hands streaked for their six-shooters. Slocum's Colt Navy bucked in his hand before Matthews got his pistol free of his belt. The Englishman stared down at the tiny red spot on his chest as if he had never seen its like before. His pistol fell from a nerveless hand and hit the ground, discharging.

Matthews dropped to his knees and looked up at Slocum. "Never thought it would end this way. Always thought an Indian would lift me scalp." He tried to laugh. Pink froth came to his lips. He wiped it away with a clumsy hand. "Got me jollies out of actin' like an Indian. Cheap barstid wouldn't give me my due..." Zebediah Matthews fell face down in the dirt.

"Reckon he meant Durant," said Marshal Haggart.

"Reckon he did." Slocum put his pistol into its holster and went to the fallen man. He rolled him over with the toe of his boot, then reached down and took the watch.

"That's what this is all about?" asked Haggart. "Son, you are a caution." Haggart reined his horse around and started back for Fargo.

Slocum held the watch to his ear and listened to the rhythmic ticking. It hadn't been damaged. He turned and walked away from Matthews's corpse. The buzzards could feast for all he cared.

Justice had been served.

19

"Lars can take care of our visitor," said Marshal Haggart, smiling broadly as he shoved Benjamin Durant into the small jail's outer office.

"I'll be out in an hour," Durant said. "And in two you'll be looking for another job."

"You might be doin' me a favor, Mr. Durant," allowed the lawman. "I been meeting some pretty lowlife folks of late. Goes with the job, maybe." He shoved Durant toward the cells in the rear of the jail. "See to him proper-like, now, Lars. Don't want him gettin' out like he did before."

The deputy silently escorted the shipping magnate toward the single remaining intact cell. Durant jerked free and spun around to face Haggart and Slocum.

"You're both dead men for this. I won't let it go. I swear!"

The door opened behind Slocum, but he didn't take his eyes off Durant.

Durant shouted, "And you, you bitch! I'll see you in hell for what you've done! You're responsible for all this! You and that whore daughter of yours!"

"Get him into the cell," Haggart said tiredly. "He's startin' to wear on my nerves." The marshal went to his desk and opened the middle drawer. A bottle of amber liquid gurgled and he lifted it out and uncorked it. "Want some of Dr. Goble's Invigorator and Nerve Remedy? No?" Haggart took a quick swig of the liquor and made a face. "Terrible stuff, but it surely does calm me down."

"John?" came Nicole's quavering voice. "Is it all over?"

"Reckon it is." Slocum faced the girl. Claudette stood behind her, one hand resting on her shoulder. He looked from one to the other and asked, "Why aren't you halfway to Winnipeg by now? Your riverboat was supposed to sail hours ago."

"The *City of Moorhead* developed boiler trouble," Claudette answered. "We had no choice but to remain. They are supposed to have it fixed by now."

Punctuating her words was a steam whistle from the docks. The *City of Moorhead* was ready to steam northward.

Unresolved questions rose within Slocum. He had his revenge; he had recovered his brother's sole legacy. But what about Nicole? The girl had been crying. Her bright blue eyes were rimmed with red and her regal, straight nose had been wiped too many times. It made her look as if she had been drinking.

"My daughter and I wanted to see that my husband —my *former* husband, that is—would not trouble us further."

"Can't say how long I can hold him, ma'am," said Haggart. "We got a good case to bring against him being the head of the fake Indian renegades robbin' the riverboats over the past couple months. Got him for breakin' jail. Would like to hang the son of a buck, but that might be out of the question."

Slocum saw the thoughts flashing across Haggart's as plain as if they had been written out. The marshal considered a lynch mob ending his woes with the shipping magnate, but John Haggart was too good a lawman to allow that. He'd keep Durant safe for the judge to pass sentence, but with Durant's wealth to buy lawyers and juries, he might not serve any time.

Fact was—and Slocum recognized this as what would probably happen—Durant would be out on the streets again in a day or two. By that time, he would be long gone. Would it be with Nicole and her mother?

"Come along, John. Please," begged Nicole. She took his hand and pulled him toward the door.

"Son, a minute," called out Haggart. When Slocum looked back at the marshal, he said, "I like you, boy. You got what I need to keep the peace in Fargo. If you want to wear a badge full time, I got a new deputy position that just opened up for you."

Slocum almost laughed. He couldn't picture himself as a deputy marshal. He knew this wouldn't last long at all. Some of the wanted posters floating around with his picture on them would eventually cross Haggart's desk. Slocum didn't want to face that future—and he just couldn't see himself as keeping the law. The very idea rankled.

"Thanks, Marshal, but I got other things pulling at me right now." He glanced at Nicole, then back.

"Remember what I said, son. Me and you, we're like peas in a pod. Now get on out of here. I got paperwork to do gettin' Mr. Durant put up proper for arraignment."

Outside in the street, Claudette said briskly, "Hurry, Nicole. The paddlewheeler will not wait for us. You know what the captain said about keeping to his schedule. We must reach Hudson's Bay by Thursday noon if we are to catch the ship for home." She turned and walked off, head held high. Slocum saw the pain in her, but she said nothing. The idea of her daughter and him together bothered her haughty nature.

"Come with us, John. I need you so." Nicole clutched at his arm and rested her head against his shoulder as they walked slowly toward the docks.

"You're going to France?"

"Mama can support us there. She still has family in

the south, and Papa can't do anything to us. You heard what he said. He . . . he's an awful man."

Slocum said nothing. He walked, lost in deep thought. By the time they reached the dock he had made his decision.

"The *City of Moorhead*'s about to sail," he said. "You'd better get aboard."

For an instant Nicole didn't understand the meaning of his words. Then she turned. He saw the icy hardness in her eyes that marked her mother.

"You're coming with me, John."

"Don't reckon I am," he said. "It would never work out. I don't belong in France. You do. At first it might be fine between us, but I'd get to hating the country and not understanding what everyone was saying."

"You could learn French. It's not that difficult."

"For you. For me . . ." He shook his head. His resolve hardened. "Go on. You belong there. I don't. By the time you came to realize that, we'd both hate each other. I'd prefer warm memories."

"They can't chase away the cold and lonely nights," she said.

"No," he said softly. "They can't."

Nicole started to argue further, then stopped. She stood on tiptoe and kissed him lightly. "I love you, John Slocum." The girl spun and dashed up the gangplank just as the roustabouts slid it on board. The steam whistle screeched again and the *City of Moorhead* pulled away from the dock. Its engines began turning the paddlewheel faster and faster. Within minutes, the boat rounded a bend in the Red River and vanished. The last sight Slocum had of it was a small figure with ash-blonde hair waving a white handkerchief from the top deck.

He cursed himself as a damned fool, then went to find a livery. He had money in his pocket and the Badlands beckoned to him. A day's ride would put him beyond Benjamin Durant's reach for good.

Besides, that was the country he belonged in. France was a world away—and would soon have a new princess reigning in it.

His princess.